Sherlock Holmes

The Skull of Kohada Koheiji
and
Other Stories

Mike Hogan

with illustrations by
Richard C Plaza

Kaleidoscope

Kaleidoscope Books
www.kaleidoscopeproductions.com

Sherlock Holmes: The Skull of Kohada Koheiji and Other Stories
Mike Hogan. – 2nd illustrated, expanded ed.
First published by MX Publications, 2015.
ISBN 9781799234128

To Mary and Bill

CONTENTS

MURDER ON THE
INFLEXIBLE

Sherlock Holmes flipped down a corner of his *Times* and regarded me across it. "What's amiss?"

I gave a guilty start as I realized I had been staring at my friend, or at least at the newspaper he had held up before him. "Nothing I would bother you with, Holmes, nothing at all, except that—"

Holmes lit his after-breakfast pipe and lifted an eyebrow. "It's just," I continued hesitantly, "I received a note this morning from a chap who was on my team at the Club, the Blackheath Rugby Club. We both studied at Bart's, but I joined the Army and he gave up Medicine, changed his degree to Theology at a small college in mid-Wales and joined the Navy as a chaplain."

"Poor chap." Holmes turned the page of his *Times* and again flicked down a corner. "And?"

"He has a billet on a ship berthed somewhere near Plymouth. He invited me to visit several times, but, I don't know, I never found the time."

"Or, judging by your tone, the inclination," said Holmes, flicking his paper up again with a languid gesture.

I hung my head. "My reluctance had to do with my erstwhile friend. I last met Hesketh (for that is his name) two years ago, and we did not find common ground. I (and he too I suspect) endured a painful evening in a coffee public house in Putney close to where he was attending a convocation of naval clergy."

"He was no longer the young man you had scrummed with at Blackheath," Holmes suggested from behind his newspaper.

"I am sure that there is no such word as 'scrummed', Holmes, but I take your meaning. I couldn't find a subject on which we could converse: not sport, not literature, not public affairs, not even the latest Gilbert and Sullivan, *The Mikado*, which he had not seen."

Holmes dropped his paper to the floor, tamped his pipe with his thumb and smiled. "Not God?"

"I say, Holmes, have a care! The thing is, his ship is now anchored in the Thames, and Hesketh is coming here."

Holmes stood and felt the toe of the Persian slipper in which he kept his tobacco. "Then I shall leave you to your reminiscences. I have one or two things to do. You are out of *Ship's* blend. I shall pass by your tobacconist in the Strand and make an order on your account. And your birthday and Christmas are in a certain number of months, so I must make my semi-annual pilgrimage to Gamages emporium for suitable scarves. And then I have a list of references to look up at the British Museum."

"It is you Reverend Hesketh wants to see, Holmes, not me." I held out the note, but Holmes waved it away. "He wants to consult you on a matter of grave urgency and delicacy," I insisted. "It is a problem of—"

The doorbell rang. I looked at my watch, stood and opened our sitting-room door. "That will be Hesketh; he is exact to his time."

Holmes folded himself into his chair with a sniff.

"Come in, my dear Hesketh," I said to a familiar figure in the black frock coat, waistcoat and white collar of a Church-of-England vicar. "Let me take your hat," I offered. "And may I introduce my friend Sherlock Holmes, the consulting detective?"

Hesketh gave me his flat-crowned clerical hat and shook hands. Holmes waved a greeting with his pipe in his casual manner as I ushered our guest to our sofa and took my place in an armchair opposite him.

Hesketh's thin, reddish hair was sparser than when I had last seen him, and he looked as corpulent and pasty-faced as he had on that occasion, but also worn and anxious.

"My ship is a first-class battleship, HMS *Inflexible*," he began in his shrill voice even before he had settled himself on the sofa. "We usually anchor in the Hamoaze at Plymouth, but a few days ago we were ordered to steam at full speed to the Thames. We arrived this morning, instantly disassembling our flying bridge, unstepping our masts and lowering our funnels before we were towed under the bridges of London to our berth near the Houses of Parliament." He pulled a handkerchief from his sleeve and mopped his brow. "I come to you in all confidence – oh dear. I hardly know where to begin."

Holmes gestured for me to pass him Hesketh's note, and he read it and raised his eyebrows. "Your vessel is infested with vampires, Reverend Hesketh," Holmes said with a cold smile. "An uncommon state of affairs aboard one of Her Majesty's battleships."

Hesketh frowned and looked down at his shoes. "I would not say infested, Mr Holmes, but we have more of the creatures than our acting captain, Commander May, is comfortable with. I took the initiative to contact you (with the very reluctant acquiescence of the commander) after a crew member was attacked and injured as he lay in his cot in the sickbay."

"Vampires," Holmes mused. "Watson, would you kindly check our Index?"

I stood and hunted along Holmes' bookshelves for the V - Z volume of his collection of scrapbooks. I pulled the thick book down and balanced it across my knees. "Victor, Voyage, Vittoria, Vanderbilt and the Yeggman, Vipers, no, we do not have an entry for vampires."

I considered. "I seem to recall the beasts are of Hungarian extraction. They feed on blood, travel at night disguised as bats, crows or other creatures of darkness and infect innocent people (comely maidens for choice) who are thus forced to join their fraternity. The preferred method for exterminating a vampire is to drive a wooden stake through the creature's heart while it sleeps in its coffin. Lord Byron's personal physician wrote a treatise—"

"Arrant poppycock," said Holmes. "Stakes through the heart, bat disguises and comely Hungarians; ineffable twaddle. We live in the nineteenth century, not the tenth, and in England not Hungary (or Scotland, Wales, Cornwall or on the moors for that matter. Such things are less easily dismissed north of Gretna Green and west of Swindon). Vampires on the Thames, ha!"

"I hope you will visit the ship and assess the situation for yourself," Hesketh said, mopping his brow again with his large white handkerchief. "If I make any attempt at a description of the incident, you will think me quite mad."

He stood. "I must return to my ship. Might I have the temerity to request your presence on the Westminster Steps at the luncheon hour, gentlemen? I am at my wits' end."

We arranged the meeting, and I saw Hesketh to the front door and waved as he set off in a cab.

I returned upstairs to our sitting room and found Holmes chuckling to himself. "Inflexible vampires, Watson – a not unamusing correlation of ideas."

"Hesketh is not amused."

He chuckled even more. "I wonder under which of the Thirty-Nine Articles of the Church of England vampires are regulated."

The journey from Baker Street to Westminster in a four-wheeler was slow and tiresome. The recent heavy rains had flooded several streets and forced traffic to jostle through side streets. Our bony nag took a deal of persuading to move at all, and the cab driver seemed content to sit on his box exchanging news with his fellows or reading his sporting paper.

We inched forward, scraping the pavement and locking wheels with other carriages, until we reached Westminster.

Holmes waited in Parliament Square while I haggled over the fare and chastised the driver for his lack of attention to his duty.

"A penny a minute, Watson and no tip," Holmes said, "his cab windows are thick with grime."

I opened my umbrella as the rain began again, and Holmes and I walked arm-in-arm under its protection down the steps to the ferry wharf beside Westminster Bridge.

HMS *Inflexible* was berthed in the centre of the fairway. Even viewed through increasingly heavy rain, the ship was impressive, with tall, brown masts and two squat funnels painted in the same colour. The black hull was high at the sharp prow and rounded stern, but much lower along the sides. Two massive circular turrets or casements occupied the main deck of the ship, placed *en echelon* so the guns could fire forward, backward and to a limited extent on the broadside. Each turret housed two wide-mouthed cannon. A vast white awning covered the deck.

I felt a tap on my shoulder and turned to find a young midshipman behind me.

"Mr Holmes and party?" he asked, saluting and shedding rain from his cap peak. "Midshipman Roke, sirs." He shepherded Holmes and me to a naval cutter, and we settled ourselves in the stern.

Roke glanced at his pocket watch and gave us a disapproving look before he ordered his crew to pull to the battleship. We weaved through a crowd of small craft with the young officer urging the rowers on.

"*Inflexible* is a fine vessel," I said.

"Sixteen-inch guns, sir, biggest in the Fleet," Roke said, recovering his good humour with youthful vivacity. "And fast –fourteen and a half knots."

"She seems broad on the beam."

"For stability, sir, and to make a steady gun platform. *Inflexible* has four sixteen-inch cannon, and 24 inches of armour along the main belt. If the French start their capers again, we'll show them what for."

We came alongside the ship, and I folded my umbrella and followed Holmes up a steep hanging staircase and on to the snowy wooden deck.

Rain drummed on the awning above us as the midshipman conducted us past the gleaming white superstructure and huge turrets, among a forest of wide-mouthed ventilators, and down a staircase into the bowels of the ship. He hurried us along steel-walled, empty corridors towards the stern of the vessel, until we stopped at a solid wooden door with a shining brass handle.

The midshipman straightened his cap, I brushed at my damp clothes with my hands, and Holmes hummed the 'Ruler of the Queen's Navee' air from *HMS Pinafore*.

"The wardroom," Roke said, in a reproving tone. He opened the door and ushered us into a carpeted room with chintz-covered armchairs set between occasional tables and clusters of aspidistra pots. Nautical scenes and portraits of naval worthies in heavy gilt frames lined the walls. Stoves warmed the room and bright oil lamps lit it. There was a pleasant smell of beeswax and Navy blend tobacco.

The half-dozen officers who stood in a group around one stove turned as we entered, and Reverend Hesketh detached himself from his colleagues and hurried across the room looking flustered.

"I am terribly sorry, gentlemen, I did not apprise you of the fact the Navy takes luncheon earlier than other mortals. It a question of a half-hour or an hour at most, but in some matters, we are punctilious to the threshold of procrusteanism."

Hesketh introduced us to the senior officer, Commander May, a florid-faced, elderly man who glanced at the clock on the wall before he nodded a greeting. The other officers were introduced in a similarly perfunctory manner as we filed into the dining room.

We clustered at one end of a long dining table laid with fine china, and white-uniformed stewards served Mulligatawny soup from silver tureens.

"Well, Mr Holmes," Commander May said as our wineglasses were filled. "Welcome to HMS *Inflexible*. I understand from our vicar that you are a detective."

"Consulting detective, if I may correct you, Commander."

Commander May stiffened, clearly unused to being contradicted.

"Could you tell us, Mr Holmes, of your recent cases?" A lieutenant whose name I could not recall asked as our soup plates were speedily removed, and the fish course served.

Holmes considered. "As I am sure you will appreciate, discretion prevents me from commenting on most of my cases, at least until the principals are no longer occupied in the matter. I can mention one recent affair in which I acted for the Lord Nelson."

"A descendant of our hero, I make no doubt?" the lieutenant suggested with what I can only characterise as a simper.

"The Lord Nelson public house in Brighton. They were troubled by spectral apparitions of its famous namesake. As one might have expected, a disgruntled potboy was behind the supposed haunting."

The officer blinked in astonishment, and the commander's face reddened. I caught Holmes' eye and gave him a warning look, but he was not in an accommodating mood. He sniffed and turned his attention to his salmon.

I smiled at Hesketh, my right-hand neighbour, and gestured at the long rows of empty chairs on either side of the table. "Many of the ship's officers are not joining us for luncheon. Are they performing a manoeuvre upstairs under the command of the captain?"

"Captain Meredith is unwell; he is recuperating on his estates in Cumberland."

"And the other officers?"

"I cannot divulge—"

"According to yesterday's *Pall Mall Gazette*," Holmes said, looking up from his plate, "HMS *Inflexible* is on the river to provide a floating reserve against the Whitechapel or Lambeth mobs should they move against the West End.

You will recall last year rioters broke the windows of clubs in St James's and looted shops. The article states most of your crew are at the Tower being drilled in infantry tactics and the use of Gatling guns."

"Damme, sir," Commander May cried, banging his fist on the table, "that is a military secret."

Holmes shrugged. "I doubt the inhabitants of the Whitechapel rookeries take the *Pall Mall Gazette*; it is far too radical for them. If your secret information appears in the *Penny Pictorial*, you have more reason for concern."

Holmes' remark was greeted with a cold silence maintained until the cloth was drawn and we were offered cigars and brandy.

Holmes cut his cigar and lit it with a match. "What of vampires, gentlemen?" he asked.

There was a long pause as each of the officers glanced at the others.

"The affair is preposterous," Commander May said at last. "I attribute the man's wounds to rats. They are ever present, even in iron ships. On *Inconstant*, I caught one as it scampered across my breast. I presented it to Prince Louis of Battenberg, who christened it the Tsar. I strangled the beast with my bare hands and had its head mounted above the desk in my cabin."

"Which ports has the ship recently visited?" I asked after another long silence.

"We were in Plymouth from January and in the Med' most of last year," Commander May said.

"Not Hungary?" I received blank looks from most of the officers. Mr Roke and two other midshipmen at the far end of our group stifled giggles.

"I do not believe Hungary proper is blessed with a coastline, Watson," Holmes said. "The Danube is navigable of course."

"I meant via the Danube, Holmes," I said stiffly.

The midshipmen heaved with barely suppressed laughter, and the older officers grinned.

Holmes stood. "If you gentlemen will excuse us, Doctor Watson and I will visit your invalid and begin our investigations. I understand the attack took place in the sickbay. Perhaps Reverend Hesketh could conduct us there?"

Hesketh requested and received permission to leave the table, and he and Midshipman Roke led us to the door.

"Rats, Mr Holmes," the commander called after us, cackling and banging the table with the flat of his hand. His fellow officers joined him in unseemly hoots of laughter.

"Fiddle faddle," Holmes muttered under his breath. "And folderol."

We followed Hesketh along gangways and down stairways to the sickbay where a young, handsome, shining-black man, as black as any man I had ever seen, lay tightly pinned by starched white sheets in a cot hanging from the ceiling. There were no other patients in the cabin.

A short, slight, middle-aged man in a white uniform stood beside the cot. "Sickbay Attendant Norris, sirs," he said in a north country accent. "The surgeon is ashore, and our only patient is Head Krooman, Breast Backstay, begging Your Honours' pardon."

I introduced myself and Holmes, and I asked to view the young man's wounds. Holmes startled everyone except me by dropping to his knees and examining the deck through his magnifying glass. "A candle, or lamp," he requested. "And open that little round window, if you will."

Norris lit a candle, put it on a saucer and laid it on the linoleum that covered the deck. He stood and opened the small scuttle, the only window in the room, allowing weak, winter sunlight and droplets of rain to stream in.

On my direction, he unwound the tight sheets pinning Backstay and revealed the patient's legs. His left foot was bound with a bloody bandage which I unwrapped, exposing two parallel wounds on his ankle each about an inch or two long and an inch apart.

"Oh, dear," said Hesketh, stepping back to the bulkhead. "I am not comfortable with the sight of blood."

"May I borrow your glass, Holmes?" I asked. He joined me in a close examination of the cuts through his magnifying glass. The penetration was not deep, but the skin had been shaved away to expose and pierce blood vessels.

"Backstay was alone in this room at the time of the attack?" Holmes asked.

"I was, sir," Backstay said in clear, unaccented English. "I am recovering from a chill." He winced as he did his best to shrug in his tightly swaddled state. "English weather is a something of a trial to persons from warmer climes."

I looked along the rows of empty cots and raised my eyebrows.

"All the other patients were sent to hospitals on shore in Plymouth when we were ordered to London," Hesketh said, following my gaze.

"But not Backstay," said Holmes.

Hesketh sniffed. "He is almost recovered from his chill."

Backstay seemed to suppress a smile.

"This attack happened last night?" Holmes asked.

"We presume so," Hesketh answered. "When Norris found Backstay this morning, he'd kicked off his bedclothes during the night (although regulations forbid it) and his foot was covered in blood. He says he felt nothing."

"Were you under any medication," I asked the man. "A sedative or roborative perhaps?"

Backstay looked to Norris. "No, sirs," the sickbay attendant answered. "Instructions was to keep the patient warm and administer beef tea at regular intervals. No medicine required. Commander May popped in late last night to offer a kind restorative for the both of us." He mimed drinking a glass. "Rum, sirs. Commander May is a fine gentleman."

Holmes indicated the scuttle in the cabin wall. "Was that window open or closed?"

"Closed last night, sir," said Norris. "And the cabin is always locked as we have spirits in the medicine cupboard." He frowned. "Brandy and rum, I mean, sir. I sling my hammock just outside the door and I heard and saw nothing. I am a light sleeper."

"No matter, a grown man could not get through that window," Holmes said. "And there is no other way in, apart from the door."

"You forget," I said. "Vampires can transform themselves into crows or other fell creatures that could wriggle through the window with ease."

Holmes smiled a thin smile.

"The rows of hooks along the sides of the sickbay," I said, "I imagine they are for cots or hammocks."

"Yes, sir," Norris answered. "We could squeeze in forty or fifty invalids, if in hammocks."

"Fifty? In this small space? Good grief. I hope you do not have a bout of gaol fever in here."

"Watson! You mustn't say such things," said Hesketh. "The men are easily spooked. We had a hygiene enthusiast visit us in Valetta last year – a German. A dozen or more seamen, some of considerable seniority, absconded when he reported we were ripe for a cholera epidemic."

We thanked Backstay and the sickbay attendant, and Hesketh led us up a series of stairs towards the upper deck with Midshipman Roke following behind.

"What is a Krooman," I asked. "And how came Backstay to have such a strange name?"

"They are men of a particular tribe recruited from Sotta Kroo on the West African coast," Hesketh answered. "We pick them up in Sierra Leone, usually in a formed group with their headman, and use them to pilot our ships along rivers and help in the suppression of the slave trade. They are handy, tough and cheerful fellows who join the ship's company for three-year's service, then return home and buy cattle and wives with their earnings."

"Backstay speaks good English," I observed.

"Indeed so. When Commander May transferred to us last year from *Inconstant*, he brought Backstay with him as a permanent supernumerary follower. I understand he was with the commander during his time with *Inconstant* on the Slave Coast."

He pursed his lips. "I believe Backstay is a prince among his own people. His Kroo name is probably unpronounceable, so he was persuaded to answer to Breast Backstay. It is our name for a certain rope up in the rigging. I am uncertain which one."

We reached the gleaming upper deck. Rain still rumbled onto the awning above us and flowed in sheets into the Thames. We stood beside one of the huge turrets.

"Who in the crew would have access to fresh blood?" Holmes asked.

Hesketh considered, his nose wrinkling in distaste. "The ship's butcher, Finnegan, and his assistants. But all the hands visit the galley to assist with food preparation or cleaning. Any one of them could acquire blood. Why do you ask?"

Holmes smiled his enigmatic smile. "Let's meet the butcher."

Hesketh gulped. "I must leave you to look up the texts for my sermon for Sunday. Mr Roke will convey you to Finnegan. Have you any clues as to the identity of the attacker, Mr Holmes?"

"Several, but I, too, must consult my authorities before moving to a conclusion."

We said our goodbyes and followed Midshipman Roke downstairs and along narrow, deserted corridors to a large, cool cabin in which whole carcasses of pigs and cows hung from ceiling hooks. The room was as brightly lit as its shore counterparts but illuminated by electric globes, rather than gas mantles.

A bushy-moustached man in filthy, brown, once-white overalls stood at a counter stirring a vat of blood. The stink of decay was far worse than the customers of any street butcher would have endured.

"Finnegan, I presume," said Holmes.

The man looked up, smiled and held out a blood-stained hand Holmes and I ignored. Finnegan chuckled and addressed us in a broad Irish brogue. "I'm making a fine black pudding for the gentlemen's breakfast tomorrow. The Commander is partial to black pudding."

"Has anyone in the crew asked you for fresh blood?" Holmes asked.

"Blood, sir? I can't think why anyone would want such an article."

"Perhaps for making a black pudding."

Finnegan folded his arms across his chest. "Any black pudding to be made on *Inflexible* is done here by my own hand. It's an art, gentlemen, getting the blood to set just right."

Holmes nodded. "Thank you, Finnegan."

We followed Midshipman Roke out of the room and back along a corridor.

Holmes stopped at the entrance to a large compartment packed with stores on shelves and bags of rice and flour heaped ceiling high. "Mr Roke," Holmes said. "I would imagine Finnegan sleeps in a separate cabin, not in the butchery."

"He messes with his assistants, the ship's painter and the leading hands."

"Show us, if you please."

Roke led us into the stores compartment. He pointed to the left side of the ship. "Yeoman of the Storerooms and other leading rates berth that side. This side we have the butcher, painter, tailor—"

"Here is where he attaches his hammock?" Holmes pointed to two sturdy hooks in the ceiling. "There are olfactory indications that suggest so."

"Sir?"

"The smell." Holmes frowned at the ceiling. "What is this little hook next to the larger one for?"

"That was where he stowed his parrot, sir, in its cage, gone now."

"I see." Holmes peered again at the small hook. "Do you have a pet, Mr Roke?"

The boy grinned and lowered his voice. "I do sir, a hamster named General Gordon. He is confined to my cabin, but I hang his cage out of the scuttle on balmy days, so he gets his fresh air."

"Very well, let us proceed upstairs."

Roke led us up onto the deck.

I was startled by a body swinging past me and a knotted handkerchief whistling past my ear.

I looked up and stepped back as a young man suspended from a line tied to a pole above our heads whirled past just above my head. The rope was attached to a wide leather strap or cummerbund wrapped around his waist, so the fellow could dangle like a circus performer, five or six feet above the deck. A circle of midshipmen and officers swatted at him with knotted handkerchiefs as he swayed above them.

"Is this corporal punishment?" I asked.

"No, no. It's a game. The midshipmen are skylarking," Roke replied. "They are playing Sling the Monkey."

Holmes and I were dropped off at the Westminster Steps. The heavy downpour had stopped, but dark-grey clouds obscured the afternoon sun and threatened more rain.

"I am astonished at the atmosphere in the wardroom of the *Inflexible*," I said as we walked to the cab rank. "The 66th Foot would not have suffered such ill-bred behaviour in the Mess, especially in front of guests. Those young whipper-snappers would have been rebuked by the chairman and beaten by the Drum Major."

"Indeed so," Holmes replied. "I am occasionally called in to consult on naval matters by my brother Mycroft, and I conceive HMS *Inflexible* is unlike any Royal Navy ship I have visited. I can only imagine, with a sickly captain, the tone of the wardroom is more a reflection of the personality of Commander May than of his superior. And she is a quiet ship; the only monkey being slung on *Inflexible* was a midshipman. I had expected a real ape or two swooping through the rigging and the usual pandemonium of parrots."

Holmes took my arm. "We have one more port of call before we settle ourselves in front of a merry fire at Baker Street."

He instructed the driver of a four-wheeler and we climbed aboard.

We followed the Strand to the City, clattered through backstreets past the Tower and turned into the Ratcliffe Highway of infamous repute.

We passed sailors' boarding houses with crossed flags or ships in full sail painted on their windows, slop shops with sou'westers and oilskins dangling in the breeze, and money exchanges with windows papered with colourful foreign currency.

Swarthy-faced men in pea jackets, print shirts and baggy trousers strolled along the pavement, many in company with ladies whose bonnets were a riot of coloured feathers and even a few flighty damsels who had dispensed with bonnets altogether.

I turned from the cab window as a thought struck me. "You inquired of the butcher whether members of the crew had asked him for blood, Holmes. Does that mean you think others have been infected?"

"Not exactly, although with his ready access to blood, a cook might thrive as a vampire. But, as you saw, Finnegan slings his hammock in the open alongside several others, and it is unlikely he could creep about, gnawing at his fellow crewmen without attracting adverse comment."

Holmes smiled. "You noted Finnegan was lying, I am sure. He has a friendly nature (as do most butchers and hangmen), yet he couldn't look me in the eye."

Holmes took out his case and offered me a cigar. "Come, Watson, you are bursting with news."

I beamed at Holmes and leaned across the cab. "Finnegan is not the only prevaricator. Backstay and Norris lied, and Reverend Hesketh may have been economical with the truth."

"The chill, ha!" Holmes said, lighting his cigar with a match and offering me a light. "Backstay winced as he shrugged. And there were the bruises."

"He was strapped up tight, Holmes," I said, puffing on my cigar. "I would guess at least one broken rib, perhaps more. The contusions were difficult to see against the colour of his skin, but his lips and an ear were unnaturally swollen. The man has been cruelly beaten."

"And he did not fight back, Watson. You saw his unmarked knuckles. Yet he is a powerful fellow. I wouldn't like to go against him in the ring. It's strange."

"Perhaps he was playing that swinging game with the midshipmen, and things got out of hand."

Holmes blew a long stream of smoke up to the ceiling of the cab. "*Inflexible* does not strike me as a ship in which members of the crew are indulged in deck games with the young officers. And note Backstay was not sent ashore to join the invalids: that is instructive. Ah, judging by the aroma, we are at Jamrach's."

The cab stopped. I opened the door, and a powerful feral stink overpowered me. I held my handkerchief over my nose as I paid the fare and I drew in a lung-full of aromatic smoke from my cigar as I turned to face the building.

The shop was a double. On the left a large plate-glass window was filled with caged birds of every size and hue. On the right was a matching window in which a host of amazing curios were displayed: bright-painted Hindoo gods, Japanese figurines of dancers, huge and curiously fluted marine shells and all manner of Oriental bric-à-brac. I was drawn to this colourful display, but Holmes coughed, and I followed him through the door next to the aviary window and into Jamrach's famous menagerie.

The room in which we found ourselves was eighteen or twenty feet square, well-lit by hanging and wall-mounted gas lamps and warmed by a stove in the centre. A counter ran around three sides, and behind it row upon row of shelves were filled with the paraphernalia of pet ownership: baskets, sacks of food, collars and leads of all descriptions, cages, paintings and photographs.

Colourful birds and small mammals occupied a line of commodious cages that stood on the counter and were affixed to the walls. Other birds fluttered free across the room or perched on the shelves. The din of whistles, shrieks and chatter beat against my ears, and a musky, animal smell assailed my nostrils.

A young clerk stood at the counter brushing the coat of a long-nosed, big-eared creature with a high-curved back and tremendous claws.

"Good morning," Holmes said. "Do you carry vampires?"

"Vampire bats, do you mean, sir? I'm afraid we are out of stock just now. If you would care to make an order, we could supply you with any number of beasts in five to six months, for sale or rent by the day, week or month."

"That is most disappointing. I had been assured you had them to hand."

"No, sir. We sold our last pair as single purchases a week or so ago. On the same day, as it happens: Wednesday."

"There, Watson. You have led me astray," Holmes said sternly. He drew on his cigar. "You assured me Jamrach's would have vampire bats in stock. You said I might rely on Jamrach's. I have come all the way from, from Edinburgh on a wild vampire chase."

"I say, Holmes—"

Holmes turned to the assistant. "I am certain one of the pair will have been purchased by Professor Blane of the Natural History Museum in Kensington. I might just be able to persuade him to lend me the creature for my exhibition at Edinburgh Zoo."

He indicated the animal on the counter. "Oddly enough, the exhibition is in aid of anteaters, particularly those of the aardvark species. We hope to obtain a breeding stock."

He put a considering finger to his lips. "But how can I be sure the purchaser of the bat was he? Professor Blane lives on the coast in Hastings. I should not like to fag out there and be disappointed."

"As I recall, sir, the animals were bought by gentlemen who gave London addresses." The clerk heaved a ledger onto the counter and flipped pages back and forth. "Yes, both customers reside in London."

"Really? I can hardly believe Professor Blane missed the opportunity to acquire a vampire bat. I should be ready to wager a half-crown or even—"

I sighed. "Might I have a look at the ledger?" I asked, and the clerk swivelled the book to face me.

"Reverend M Turner of Amoy Cottage, Peter's Lane in Clerkenwell, and R Rackstraw of 22a, Coral Street, Lambeth." I pencilled the names and addresses on my shirt cuff. "Thank you very much."

"Reverend Turner was a corpulent person, in a—" Holmes began.

"Did you serve either of the purchasers?" I asked the assistant.

"I did."

"Could you describe them?"

"Reverend Turner was a stooped, elderly man, very quiet, in clerical dress with a full, grey moustache and beard. Mr Rackstraw was shorter and clean-shaven, a rather thin fellow. I should mention I reduced the price of the bat by a percentage and took a small monkey from Mr Rackstraw in part exchange. It was not a wise decision."

"May we view the monkey?" I asked.

The clerk showed Holmes and me through a back door into the very extensive storage areas of the menagerie. He led us past shrieking, chattering parrots in all the colours of the rainbow and along a line of cages holding beasts of all types from lions to gorillas. The stink was tremendous, held at bay to an extent by our cigars. The young man stopped at a small cage high on one side in which a small, mournful-looking monkey crouched.

"Tiddles," the clerk called, "hello, Tiddles." The monkey ignored him. "Really, these Barbary Macaques are a drug on the market. I took pity on the man as he said if I he could not find a home for Tiddles, he would be destroyed."

We followed the clerk back to the shop, and Holmes strode towards the door. The aardvark on the counter twitched its long ears and gazed at me with a soulful expression as I paused and thanked the young man.

"And the vampire bat order, sir?" the clerk asked.

"We shall discuss our needs in the matter of vampires and make a decision in due course," I said. "By the way, do the bats you sold have names?"

"They are Gog and Magog."

"Outrageous," Holmes said as we stood on the pavement outside Jamrach's and puffed our cigars. "We should complain to the manager. That clerk should not give out his customers' addresses to perfect strangers in such an offhand manner. I expected to have to worm the information from him by a subterfuge. I deduced, from the copy of the Pink 'Un sporting newspaper in his jacket pocket he was a betting man; that he was an aardvark-fancier was obvious from the way he – you are not listening, Watson."

I wrote on a sheet from my notebook. "I am composing a return-paid telegram to Reverend Turner of Amoy Cottage, Peter's Lane, Clerkenwell. We can find a boy to take it to the telegraph office while we have a pint of ale at the Jolly Sailor public house over there."

Holmes and I refreshed ourselves in front of a lively fire in the public bar as we waited for a reply to my telegram. A half hour later, a telegraph boy appeared at the door and called my name. I took the telegram and read that Reverend Turner would be pleased to receive us at any time in the late afternoon.

The weather was uncertain, so we engaged a four-wheeler to Clerkenwell where we were set down in a narrow street near Smithfield meat market.

Reverend Turner, who fitted the Jamrach's clerk's description of a stooped, elderly, genial man, met us at the door of his cottage and waved us inside.

"Do come in, Mr Holmes and Doctor Watson. I have some fine Abernethy biscuits to go with our tea."

We followed the old gentleman along a narrow corridor and into a cosy sitting room with a low, thick-beamed ceiling. He ushered us to cane chairs in front of a bright fire and bustled with the kettle and tea urn. I looked around the room expecting to see a cage.

"Where does the creature live?" I asked.

"You refer to Magog?" Reverend Turner pointed to a beam in the low ceiling. "He hangs there, during the day." He passed me tea as Holmes and I exchanged alarmed looks.

"Vampire bats hunt at night, but the dear fellow is still a little confused by our dismal English afternoons. He is having a snack as we speak. I keep pigs, you see, in the backyard."

Holmes and I drew our feet up and our eyes flicked around the room in alarm.

"Both the hairy-legged vampire bats and white-winged bats prefer the blood of birds," Reverend Turner continued, "but common vampire bats, like Magog, feed on the blood of mammals (occasionally including humans)."

He smiled. "When the common vampire locates a host, such as a sleeping mammal, it lands and approaches it on the ground using its wing members as feet. It walks in a charming, jolly swagger, like a sailor just home from a distant voyage." Reverend Turner demonstrated the walk and laughed. "You'll take milk?"

I shook my head and picked up my teacup with, I am ashamed to admit, a quivering hand.

"The bat identifies a warm spot on the skin to feed from," Reverend Turner continued, "creates slits in the flesh with its incisors and laps up blood from the wound. Lump sugar, gentlemen, biscuits?"

Holmes paled and refused the offered biscuits. I took one but found that I was too dry-mouthed to consume it.

Reverend Turner settled himself in a chair by the fire. "My vampire acclimatised to its new home remarkable quickly. I understood from Jamrach's he was one of a pair kept as pets by a Cornish bishop who had to dispose of them when he married and his new wife found them surplus to the requirements of domestic contentment. Magog is perfectly tame, he will allow himself to be petted and stroked, and he comes when called – ah, here he is, the devil."

A hideous, big-eared, red-mouthed creature scuttled into the room and moved swiftly towards the fire using its feet and the tiny claws on its wingtips. It made a click, click sound on the wooden floor as it moved that ceased as it crossed the hearthrug. I was the more uncomfortable at its silent approach.

"Magog is a large specimen of the species, eight or nine inches in height," Reverend Turner explained with a smile.

The beast stood, swaying, with its head cocked to one side, and regarded me with worrying interest.

Reverend Turner leaned down and scratched it behind the ear. "Vampire bats, like most bats, are sociable animals. Magog loves to be petted, and especially to be relieved of fleas. The problem is that he rewards my attentions by offering me regurgitated blood – oh, I say, Doctor, are you quite well?"

The bat spread its wings, flapped up above our heads and hooked itself, upside down, from the beam with its head on a level with mine. It turned to face me and seemed to smile as a tiny red droplet dripped from its fangs onto my biscuit plate.

We made our excuses and retreated to the waiting cab.

"To the Waterloo Road, Cabby," said Holmes.

We settled ourselves inside the four-wheeler as rain slashed against the windows. Holmes offered me a cigarette. "Magog seems content in his new home, Watson. I see no reason for him to forsake it in favour of HMS *Inflexible*."

"Nor I," I said as I lit my cigarette with a trembling hand.

We stepped down onto the pavement opposite the Royal Victoria Hall coffee public house on the Waterloo Road and into a cold drizzle.

I paid the driver, and Holmes checked the house numbers in Coral Street. "No, as I suspected, it's a false trail. There is no such address as 22a, Coral Street, Lambeth. Good, we are getting somewhere. Now, why did our Mr R Rackstraw choose this particular non-address?"

"He knows the area," I suggested, shivering in the chill wind.

"You are sharp today, Watson, despite the dull weather. Yes, and we may also assume his name is as false as his lodgings. R Rackstraw: does it conjure any connotations for you?"

"*Pinafore!*"

"Ralph Rackstraw is the sailor in love with the Captain's daughter in the Gilbert and Sullivan operetta. So, let's see."

Holmes looked around. "I suggest we fortify ourselves against the cold with hot rum punch and perhaps something to satisfy the inner man."

Holmes led the way across the road to the Duke of Sussex public house. He ordered our drinks and chatted with the barman while I sat at a table by the fire. He joined me and passed me a welcome glass of hot punch.

"Well, Holmes, did you discover anyone in the vicinity who owns a vampire bat?"

"I did not inquire upon that subject. It would be a strange household, would you not agree, that will not admit a monkey, but accepts a vampire bat? The potboy recommends the sausages."

Holmes and I spent a pleasant interlude at the Duke of Sussex sitting by a merry fire and enjoying an excellent meal of grilled sausages with mashed potato and onion gravy before we caught a hansom and made for home.

The lamps were being lit, and the reek of fog was in the air. The first filthy tendrils of vapour wrapped around the street lamp outside our front door.

Mrs Hudson provided us with a late supper of toasted cheese, and after a desultory chat about the day's events in front of our sitting-room fire, Holmes and I said our goodnights.

It seemed only a moment later I was awakened by Holmes hammering on my bedroom door and desiring me to join him at once in our sitting room.

I put on my dressing gown and slippers, went downstairs feeling bleary-eyed and dozy, and found Roke, the young midshipman from the *Inflexible*, pale-faced and shivering by our cold fireplace.

The clock struck the half hour: it was five thirty on a dank, chilly morning with the previous night's foul miasma still tainting the air.

Holmes came from his bedroom, drying his face with a towel. He picked a folded note from the table and handed it to me.

"This is from Hesketh," he said. "He writes the vampire has struck again and asks us to come at once."

"Good Lord, Holmes. What the Devil is going on?"

"Language," Mrs Hudson said from the doorway. "This is a Christian house, Doctor. Will you be requiring coffee?"

"It's Commander May," Roke said in a trembling voice, "he's dead."

I woke Billy and sent him to fetch a four-wheeler. By the time I had washed and dressed, Mrs Hudson had produced a pot of fresh coffee that Holmes, Roke and I drank most gratefully.

The ride to Westminster was faster at that early hour, and we managed a fine pace through empty, puddled streets. Holmes sat next to me deep in thought, and Roke, sitting opposite, was pallid and anxious. I questioned him on the attack, but all he could say was the commander's body had been discovered in his cabin earlier in the morning; he knew nothing else of value.

The boat's crew quickly extinguished cigarettes and pipes and stood to their posts as our cab clattered onto the landing.

They rowed us to the huge battleship that now appeared not only powerful, but dark and menacing in the weak light from the lampposts on shore and the few oil lamps in her rigging.

Holmes and I hurried aboard and followed Roke aft to the officers' accommodation. The door of what I presumed was the commander's cabin lay open, and Hesketh and another officer stood outside.

"Thank you for coming," Hesketh said, wringing his hands. "This is our next senior, Lieutenant Bower."

Holmes pushed past the officer into the cabin, and I followed. Commander May lay in his cot as tightly bound with bed sheets and blankets as the Krooman had been. His face was marble white, unlike the ruddy-cheeked man we had met at luncheon.

Holmes cautioned me to remain at the door while he knelt and examined the linoleum that covered the floor through his glass. He stood and glared around the cabin. "The ventilator grill is a possibility."

Holmes leaned across the body to examine a perforated brass plate in the wall just above the head of the bed. "Nothing. But look here, Watson."

I joined him, and he directed my attention to the left side of the neck of the corpse. I saw two cuts an inch apart, the same incisions as those in Backstay's legs. Holmes handed me his magnifying glass, and I examined the wounds. To my astonishment, within each was a round puncture, deep into the blood vessel.

"They pierce the external carotid artery," I said. "He must have bled most profusely; in fact, he has been exsanguinated. Yet, not a drop of blood is on the bedclothes or on the floor. Was Commander May killed elsewhere and transported here?"

Holmes shook his head. "Check the body for signs of violence, will you? Particularly the knuckles."

Holmes turned to Lieutenant Bower, standing with Hesketh in the doorway. "You mopped up the blood and washed the body."

"We can't have nasty blood all over the deck, sir," the Lieutenant exclaimed. "I ordered the cabin swabbed and the commander's body cleaned as soon as the sick-berth attendant pronounced the gentleman dead."

Holmes gave me a despairing look. He bent over the commander's body, placed his hands on his chest and pressed down with all his might.

"I say, sir," Bower cried.

Holmes leaned over the face of the corpse, sniffed and stood. "Do you smell anything, Watson?"

I bent forward, took a deep breath and shook my head.

"It's a mere whiff," Holmes said. "And it may be too familiar for you to particularise."

He turned back to Lieutenant Bower. "Who found the body?"

"Sick-Birth Attendant Norris, sir. Commander May had not been quite himself since luncheon, and Norris gave him a sleeping draught. He checked on the Krooman at three or so in the afternoon, and then on the Commander to see if the draught had been effective."

"The little round window was closed, as it is now?"

"The scuttle? I'm sure the Commander would not have opened it in this weather."

Holmes steepled his fingers and tapped his lip. "Well, let's visit the sickbay. There is nothing more here."

Something caught my eye as I followed Holmes out of the cabin, and I nudged his elbow, indicating a tiny rat head mounted above Commander May's desk. "The Tsar," I whispered.

He nodded. "What of the commander?"

"Bruised knuckles," I answered. "He has been in a brawl."

Hesketh led us back to the sickbay where Backstay lay cocooned again, wide-eyed and distressed, whether in grief, in guilt or anxious for his safety, I could not tell.

Norris boiled water for coffee on a spirit stove.

Holmes addressed him. "Commander May was a popular officer?"

Norris glanced up at Hesketh and across to Backstay before he replied. "He was a Navy man, through and through, sirs. A stickler, you might say, but he'd do anything for the ship. Came up through the hawse-hole, he did. He joined as a boy seaman in the Crimean War and worked his way through to a commission and the rank of commander."

Holmes turned to Hesketh. "On the last ship I visited, there were parrots in the rigging and monkeys swinging aloft. I had thought it customary for the men to be allowed pets, but I saw none on our visit to *Inflexible* this afternoon."

"The Commander did not approve of pets, Mr Holmes," Hesketh said. "At least, he was uncomfortable with those that fouled the deck. He banned all pets after Captain

Meredith was taken ill and went home to the North. Commander May was very solicitous concerning the deck."

"It is almost white," I said.

"Your qualification of white with 'almost' would have struck Commander May to the heart," Hesketh said. "He desired perfection. But what can be flawless in this world of sin? Only in the Hereafter can purity and rightness be attained."

"Quite," I answered.

Norris handed us mugs of steaming, excellent coffee, each with a nip of rum against the chill. He freed Backstay from his sheets enough for him to sit up and sip his brew.

"How are you feeling, Mr Backstay," Holmes asked. "I am sorry to see your chill has gone to your chest, lips and left ear."

"Well enough, sir. A little tremulous after the events of the night."

"Perfectly understandable. You were Commander May's follower, were you not? You were brought into *Inflexible* when the Commander joined last year."

"That is so. I served with him in *Inconstant*, in *Raleigh* and all along the Slave Coast. Seven years in all."

"A considerable time," said Holmes. "I understand Admiralty regulations call for a three-year contract for Kroomen – is it not so, Reverend Hesketh?"

Hesketh blinked and said nothing.

"I am a supernumerary member of the *Inflexible*'s company, Mr Holmes," Backstay said. "I do not draw victuals or pay. Commander May met my expenses from his personal funds."

Holmes nodded. "You will want to pay your respects to your patron."

"I would, sir."

"Can you walk?"

Backstay heaved himself out of the cot and lowered his legs to the deck. "If I might have a stick to lean on and a pair of slippers?"

Norris produced slippers, a dressing gown and crutches from a cupboard.

"Good," said Holmes. "I suggest Norris and Reverend Hesketh accompany Backstay to the commander's cabin. He may need time to complete his observances."

Norris helped Backstay out of the cabin.

Holmes pulled Hesketh aside. "Keep Backstay and Norris busy for thirty minutes, or more if you can. Let Backstay have whatever he needs. It is of vital importance Norris and he not come back here before that time. Do you understand?"

"I do not," Hesketh answered. "But I will do as you ask. I cannot issue orders, but I have a certain spiritual authority." He frowned, shuddered and went pale. "Is Backstay a member of the Christian community? I cannot condone any heathen practices—"

Holmes ushered him out of the door and closed it. "I have a job for you too, Midshipman Roke."

The boy's face brightened.

"You must go to the butcher's cabin and request him to fill a cup with fresh cow or pig blood. You will say it's for the sickbay, and you may give him a wink if you choose. The butcher is up and about, I would assume."

The boy nodded unhappily as Holmes took a small bowl from the top of a cupboard and gave it to him. "You may run but try not to spill blood on your uniform; it's the very devil to get out."

Holmes closed the door behind the midshipman and rubbed his hands together. "Now, we must light up the cabin, Watson. Light every lamp. I will hunt the cupboards for candles."

We lit all the oil lamps and a dozen or more candles before Holmes knelt on the linoleum and bade me squat beside him. "You see in the bright light? I could not make it out this afternoon in the gloom: a trail of pinpricks in the linoleum. You will recall similar marks made in Reverend Turner's thin hearthrug in only the few days that Magog has been with him. Our trail leads to and from the ventilator in the cabin wall. The grill covering the hole is held by one screw, not the regulation four. It swings open – oiled you notice." He flipped the grating cover open and shut.

We stood. I took out my cigar case and offered him one.

"No, Watson, we must not smoke for a while. Another coffee perhaps?"

"You made a point of Backstay's connection with the commander, Holmes. Do you suspect the Krooman of the murder?"

Holmes tapped his lip with a finger in a characteristic gesture. "Backstay could have returned to his people after finishing his three-year contract. Yet, he and Commander May were together for seven years aboard three ships. He is, what, twenty now? He was a mere boy when he joined. He stayed beyond his term for a reason: loyalty perhaps or hope of advancement."

"How came he by his injuries?"

"Commander May beat him," said Holmes.

"Monstrous!" I exclaimed. "What naval punishment would break ribs? How dare he inflict such injury on a member of the crew!"

"Backstay is not technically a member of the crew. He is a personal follower of Commander May who transferred with his patron from ship to ship. The commander payed his expenses. I would expect that an affection has grown between the boy and —"

"I say, Holmes, are you suggesting an unnatural—"

"No, no, I sense the commander's feelings towards Backstay were paternal. We saw over luncheon May has an irascible temperament, but some of the most petulant men I know are indulgent fathers."

"Could he be May's son?" I mused. "His complexion argues against it."

"Not a father by blood, but perhaps he offered fatherly protection to the boy; such connections are not uncommon in the Navy."

"As we have said, Holmes, Backstay is a powerful youth. If you are right, and Commander May beat him viciously, then why did he not defend himself?" I asked.

"Something stayed his hand: again, affection or loyalty come to mind. Commander May was a brute, but many a violent father has doting sons."

"But you suspect Backstay of murdering his patron under the guise of a vampire attack?"

Holmes smiled a wan smile. "We know that love and hate are but two sides of the same coin – ah, here is Roke, unspotted I see, well done."

Holmes took the bowl of blood from the Midshipman and placed it carefully on the deck.

"Snuff the candles and all but one lamp," he ordered. He flipped the grating open and whistled into the opening.

"Gog," he cooed, "breakfast time, my dear. Come and get your lovely blood."

I turned down the last lamp and heard a soft scuttling sound that raised the hairs on the back of my neck. The vampire bat that emerged from the ventilator opening was just as ugly as Reverend Turner's Magog, but about a third shorter. Midshipman Roke gasped and leapt onto the counter, and I leaned forward to get a closer look.

"That creature killed a senior commander in Her Majesty's Royal Navy?" I said with a sniff. "I find it hard to believe."

"Even naval Commanders have carotid arteries, Watson. Although I admit, the beast seems docile, or at least, not particularly ferocious."

The bat scuttled across the deck in a strange, staggering gait and bent over the bowl.

"It laps like a cat," said Holmes, "but judging from the mess it makes on the floor, it has not the cat's fastidious table manners."

The beast finished its meal and looked up at us, licking its fangs and dribbling blood.

"Gog wishes to be petted, Watson. Scratch it behind the ears."

The bat lurched to one side and bumped into the cabinet under Roke's counter. The Midshipman drew his dirk and cowered against the cabin wall.

"Ha," I said. "Did you add a rum restorative to the blood, Holmes? The beast is unsteady on its pins."

The bat seemed to rest against the cabinet for a moment, then it shook its head and staggered forward with its mouth open, revealing razor-sharp incisors dripping with pink foam. It blinked at us in what might have been, had the beast been an aardvark, a mournful manner.

"Shoo, shoo," I exclaimed, waving my folded umbrella at the bat; it bristled, gnashed its teeth and flopped on its side.

"I believe you have alarmed it, Watson," said Holmes. "Let's light the lamps and encourage it to return to its lair."

Midshipman Roke and I frantically lit candles and lamps. The beast hissed in a reproving manner, heaved itself up on its claws and scuttled unsteadily back through the grating into the ventilator. Holmes closed it with a click. He placed the creature's feeding bowl on top of a cupboard and wiped the blood spots from the floor with a cloth.

I breathed more easily and judging by his complexion Midshipman Roke breathed for the first time since the creature had appeared.

The cabin door opened and Hesketh entered with Backstay and Norris behind him.

"We saw the vampire," Roke cried, jumping down from the counter.

"Can it be tracked to its lair?" Hesketh exclaimed. "Should we call in a White Hunter? Or perhaps an exorcist?"

"It's not a man-eating lion," Holmes said. "Nor yet a Hungarian ghoul. Commander May was not killed by a vampire, he was deliberately murdered by a human rather than chiropteran agency. The penetration marks on Commander May's neck were additional to the scraping marks the bat made. The similarity of the twin pricks in the commander's wounds to the fictional descriptions of vampire bites suggests a human, not a beastly or ghoulish, agency."

Midshipman Roke looked at him in confusion.

"Holmes suggests a bat didn't kill Commander May, a man did so," I said. "Mr Norris, might I prevail on you to make us more of your excellent coffee?"

Roke gave a vivid description of Gog's appearance to Backstay and Hesketh as Norris made coffee and passed around mugs. He unlocked the spirits cupboard and reached up to a shelf lined with rum and brandy bottles. Holmes spilled a little of his hot coffee onto his sleeve, cried out, staggered and fell against Norris. The man screeched and backed to the side of the cabin holding his left arm tenderly with his right.

"Dear me," said Holmes. "You have a sore arm, Norris."

Norris glared fearfully at Holmes. "Which, I bruised it on a stanchion in the January storms."

"You should have reported your injury, Norris," Hesketh said. "You of all people should know the regulations."

"Beg pardon, sir," Norris said, casting a venomous glance at Holmes.

"Watson and I were sorry to hear you had to part with Tiddles, Norris," Holmes said. "The poor creature still misses you terribly, is that not right, Watson?"

"Indeed. It is evident in his sad demeanour and lack of appetite, poor fellow."

Norris glared from Holmes to me, then his eyes glistened. "Commander May ordered me to get rid of my monkey," he said in a voice quivering with emotion. "Tiddles, what had been with me from a pup. He said he fouled the deck, which he never did."

"You sold him to Jamrach's," Holmes said.

"It was that or put him down!" Norris cried, tears streaming down his face. "I tried to give Tiddles his freedom, like, and let him loose in a park in Plymouth, but he found his way back to me, the little mite, and Commander May said he must go."

Norris wiped his eyes with his sleeve. "Commander May kept his pet darkie, Backstay, but I had to put my Tiddles down."

"You went ashore and got another little pet," Holmes said, sipping his coffee. "Watson gave Gog his breakfast, a scratch behind the ears and sent him back to his lair in the ventilator."

He smiled. "Your arm was injured when you let the creature feed from you before you suborned the butcher to your plan. He had lost his pet parrot to the new regulations, and he was willing to cooperate and provide you with blood. When Backstay was brought to the sickbay after a beating from Commander May – what was the reason for that, Backstay?"

"I went with the lads to a Judy house on shore," the Krooman answered. "The commander warned me against the pox. I laughed, and he lost his temper. He was main sorry when he saw what he'd done. He was a hard man, but kindly in his way. He looked on me as a son, and I him as a father."

Holmes nodded. "When you were admitted to the sickbay, Norris put his plan into operation. He no doubt chloroformed you, had Gog feed on you, and then he spread the word a vampire was loose on the ship."

"The smell," I said. "The taint in May's cabin; it was chloroform."

"Gog was purchased by Norris as cover for deliberate murder," Holmes continued, "revenge for Commander May's edict against pets. Against Tiddles."

Norris blinked through his tears at Holmes. "I done the commander and I wish I could do him again."

He giggled, opened a drawer and took out a smooth silver pellet. "Commander May said he had the gripes after lunch, so I gave him the ship's antimonial pill, what made him sick with the runs. I nursed him all evening like he was my firstborn. Ha! He was main grateful. He said he'd look into my rate and maybe get me a leg up in promotion, the bugger."

Norris rummaged in the drawer again and produced a fork. The middle tine had been removed, and the remaining two were sharpened to razor points. "I chloroformed him and set Gog to him. Then I bled him out while he was under the ether. It didn't take long. I kept some blood for—"

Backstay lunged towards Norris but was held back by Roke and Hesketh.

"How would you compare Gog with his charming companion Magog?" Holmes asked me. "Did he not seem lacking in *joi-de-vivre*, in vim and in vigour? Was he not a little unsteady on his claws, and less genial than his friend in Clerkenwell?"

"Perhaps cow's blood does not suit its taste, or – oh, good Lord, Holmes! The beast is sick. I am no veterinarian, but the symptoms are, let me see, somnolence, partial paralysis, confusion, foaming at the mouth and alternating fawning and aggressive behaviour. If it is the fell disease I believe you suspect—"

Holmes nodded gravely.

I turned to Norris and shook my head. "If you allowed your pet to feed from you, I regret to inform you that you are a dead man. We have reason to believe your bat is suffering from rabies."

Norris' eyes widened, and he backed against the cabin wall. Backstay dropped his crutches and struggled in the grip of Hesketh and Roke, roaring in his native language.

I turned to him. "Now I come to think of it, I am very much afraid you are both doomed."

Backstay yanked himself loose with a great cry. He pulled a heavy surgical cleaver from a rack against the wall and grabbed Norris by the hair. He held the cleaver high.

"Don't," I exclaimed. "Norris is a dead man, I guarantee it. There is no cure for rabies."

"Then so am I fated, Doctor," said Backstay. "It is a bad way to die. I've not seen men die in a worser way."

I nodded. "But you have a little longer. The farther the wound is from the head, the more the symptoms are delayed."

Backstay thought on that, and he threw Norris to the deck. "I hope he squeals in agony before the end."

"You might find a screwdriver in Norris's drawer," said Holmes. "We should screw the grill tight shut. There will be a nasty smell in the ventilators in a day or two."

"My God!" cried Hesketh. I turned as he slumped to the deck in a faint. Backstay sat against the cabin wall beside him smiling, the surgical cleaver in his hand. His left leg lay before him in a growing pool of blood, clean cut off at the knee.

I was hunting along the line of index books above Holmes' desk in our sitting room after breakfast the next morning when Billy appeared at the door and handed me a pair of telegrams.

"A message from Clerkenwell, Holmes. Magog is thriving and showing no signs of illness. He sends his regards. Another from Hesketh on *Inflexible* saying the same of the Krooman prince."

I frowned. "How did you know Norris had purchased the vampire bat under the name of Rackstraw?"

"I enquired at the Sussex Arms pub in Lambeth."

"You told me you had not asked that exact question," I said sternly.

"I did not enquire about a vampire bat. I asked the potboy if he knew someone with a tame Macaque monkey named Tiddles. He identified Norris as a sailor who lived with his mother in the Hercules Road." He smiled at me. "What is an antinomial pill?"

"It's a plug of metallic antimony that is swallowed as an emetic. The pill is not ingested by the body, and it loses only a tiny fraction of its mass, if any, as it passes through the stomach and intestines. It's recovered and used again. Antinomial pills are handed down from generation to generation of a family, or in this case the members of a ship's company."

"How disgusting." Holmes sat at his desk, a pot of glue and a pile of newspaper and magazine clippings before him.

"By the way, I'd try Scull's Greek Myths, rather than the Index, Watson, but I can save you the trouble. Procrustean derives from Procrustes, an Attic Greek bandit who invited travellers to sleep on his iron bed. Those too short were forcibly stretched, those too tall were cut to fit. He is the patron of the rigid enforcement of arbitrary rules. He suffered the fate he had visited on innocent travellers when he was caught by King Theseus and stretched (some say pruned) on his own bed. There, I have updated the 'V to Z' index regarding vampires, real and ghostly."

I looked over his shoulder at a sketch of a vampire bat and shuddered. "Gog and Magog belong to a species named the *common* vampire bat, Holmes. I don't like the sound of that. I'll have Billy put up the shutters."

THE RATCLIFFE HIGHWAY AFFAIR

It was a dismal morning in late November, the wind howled, snow drifted thick in Baker Street, a hansom was down with its horse sprawled on the icy road just outside our front door, and I was obliged to open the window.

"Holmes, I must protest."

"What?"

"Mrs Hudson has asked me to make representations on her behalf: it will not do."

Holmes looked up from his experimental bench and shook his head. "A man's life may—"

"That's what you always say when you stink us out of house and home with your vile chemicals. My dear fellow, it will not do."

Holmes slapped down his magnifying glass. "On your head it must be then, Doctor Watson. On your head must it be." He placed a test tube of clear liquid in a stand and picked up a sliver of paper.

"You have been following the Sanderson poisoning trial in the newspapers? If this litmus paper turns blue, he faces the hangman, if red, he is a free man."

He dipped the slip of paper into the chemical solution; it changed colour.

"It's purple, Holmes," I said, not without a certain inner glee. "Neither blue, nor red. What then?"

He pursed his lips as he considered. "Perhaps he was an accessory to the deed. He must have had accomplices."

I sat in my usual seat by the fire and picked up the *Pall Mall Gazette*. "You treat your chemicals and phials as an alchemist of a past age would his crucibles and crystal ball. I'm surprised you don't read the future through your magnifying glass or play the oracle with the stains on your workbench."

Holmes turned away without a word, and I was put out of countenance. I had been brusque, but Holmes' bohemian habits were a trial to the household, especially when we were confined at home by winter storms.

I tried to think of a way to re-establish domestic cordiality as Mrs Hudson bustled into the sitting room with the breakfast tray followed by Billy with the coffee and post.

Mrs Hudson sniffed, coughed, laid the table in a determined manner that spoke volumes and slammed the window closed.

Breakfast was a subdued affair as Holmes and I ate our kippers, read our mail and buried ourselves in our respective newspapers. Each of us declared politely the other should take the last piece of toast and it was left cold and forlorn, much like the day and our usually convivial friendship.

I lit my after-breakfast pipe as Holmes slipped a cigar from my packet on the mantelpiece.

"My dear fellow," he said as he regarded the packet with disdain. "A shilling for three cigars. Your man in the Strand offers fine Panatelas at two and six for three that are ambrosia to the gods. I will refuse to borrow your cigars if you continue to purchase cheap and inferior brands."

I grunted a reply. Holmes was endeavouring to restore amiability, but my leg ached in the chill weather, and I was in no mood for repartee. However, after ten minutes of silence, I made an effort at conversation as Billy cleared the breakfast table.

"Here is something that might interest an inquiring mind, Holmes. Here is a phenomenon that would tax even the detective skills of the great criminologist Alphonse Bertillon."

"Pshaw," Holmes said with a sniff. "He is much over-rated."

"The *Pall Mall Gazette* suggests a spirit is abroad in Limehouse, inhabiting a house on the Ratcliffe Highway and telling fortunes. It picked the winner of the Triple Crown and Champion Stakes and it predicts war with Russia next season."

"Ormande," said Billy.

Holmes and I looked blankly at the boy, and he coloured bright pink. "It was in the Doctor's newspaper. The winning horse in the Stakes—"

"I will not have you reading my newspaper before you bring it up to me," I said much more vehemently than I had intended. "It disarranges the pages and makes creases and, um—"

Billy looked up at me with astonishment, and Holmes regarded me with raised eyebrows over a corner of his *Times*.

"I am sorry, Billy," I said. "I spoke intemperately. The thought of the poor deluded fools who flock to fortune-telling charlatans made me rather, that is, somewhat vexed."

I glanced at Holmes. "It would be a public service if someone were to expose the fraudsters and drive them from the city."

Holmes returned to his newspaper. "I see the young Lord Crampton, the only son of the late Marquis of Rawley, is still missing in Upper Burma. It has been almost three months since his cavalry piquet was ambushed by Burmese bandits and no trace of him has been found."

"I only looked at the newspaper while I ironed it for the Doctor," Billy murmured in an aggrieved tone as he cleared the breakfast table. "Can't get so much as a thank-you in this house, not if things are ever so."

He carried the laden tray to the door, making a fuss of opening it with his elbow and edging out.

I sighed in exasperation, and Holmes flicked down his newspaper again and peered over it.

"My dear fellow, we have been cooped up in the house treading on each other's toes and getting hot under the collar for almost a week. Come, we mustn't let this long spell of inclement weather imprison us. I see the sun is peeping out. Billy will get us a cab, a four-wheeler in view of the snow."

Holmes waved his newspaper at Billy in the doorway. "Fetch a growler, one with a sturdy horse mind, none of your boneyard specimens. We've a way to go."

"Where are we going, Holmes?" I asked.

"Upper Burma."

I looked at him in astonishment.

"By way of the Ratcliffe Highway. Bring your stethoscope."

"I know that awful stench, Holmes," I said as our cab stopped outside the Jolly Sailor public house on the Ratcliffe Highway, newly rechristened, officially at least, St George's Street East.

"It is the aroma of baboons."

A police constable stood outside the door of the public house, and Holmes beckoned him to the cab. "We are looking for the Ratcliffe Oracle, Constable. Could you direct us?"

The policeman looked blankly at him.

"They want the Voice," the cabby called down from his perch on the box at the front of the four-wheeler.

"Oh, the Voice is it?" the constable answered. "That's up by the Crown and Dolphin in Cable Street."

"I know that," the cabby replied. "How would I not know where the Crown and Dolphin is, me what was born and brought up not two streets away? Answer me that, eh?"

He flicked the reins, and we jerked into a trot, leaving the policeman with no right of reply.

"That showed the bugger," the cabby muttered. "The bleeding fare should give exact addresses as is right and proper under the Parliamentary Act and not mess about with Ratcliffe this and Jolly Sailor that when it's the Crown and Dolphin and the bleedin' Voice he wants."

I blinked at Holmes and put my handkerchief over my nose as the odour intensified. Holmes pointed out of the window to a long grey building with shuttered windows. "You will recall Jamrach's menagerie from the *Inflexible* affair. Jamrach's advertises in *The Times* that baboons are in season again at twelve guineas the pair."

Ten minutes later, the cabs wheels screeched against the edge of the pavement as the cabby stopped in Cable Street.

"The Crown and Dolphin," he said. "Three and a tanner."

We stepped carefully down on to the icy pavement, and I paid the driver. He looked at the coins in his palm with disdain. "Gents could have saved thruppence had we gone direct. Throwing money in the gutter, I don't know."

The cab clattered away, and we saw before us a row of three buildings: the Crown and Dolphin public house on the corner of Cable Street and Cannon Street Road, then a thin, grimy building with boarded-up windows, and completing the row on the right an equally dark and filthy house advertising a gimcrack carnival show.

Outside the public house a fiddler bundled in so many coats he appeared almost spherical played light airs, and a small group of vendors (religious tracts, matches, and bootlaces from what I could see) huddled around a brazier, stamping their frozen feet in time with the music. An enticing aroma of grilled sausages wafted along the street until it was overpowered by the stink of horse dung.

Despite the cold, a queue of a dozen people stood in the slush outside the door of the middle house, all low women in layer upon layer of coats and with patched shawls over their bonnets. They peered through the black-curtained windows of the house, breathing on the glass and rubbing it with their sleeves.

The door opened, and four women came out and pushed through the crowd, chattering excitedly, and a tall, thin man in a long overcoat and bowler leaned out of the door and called four more women forward.

A gleaming, closed private carriage pulled up, and the man held up his hand and waved the women away.

The crowd stood aside as two footmen in blue greatcoats unfolded the carriage steps and opened the door for a young, fashionably dressed woman who stepped down, turned and helped an elderly lady out of the carriage and across the icy pavement.

Holmes watched with pursed lips as they were ushered into the house by the thin man.

"The coat of arms on the carriage door is obscured, and the footmen and drivers have no insignia on their coats. The marchioness does not wish to be recognised."

The door closed, and the women outside the house huddled again at the windows.

Holmes turned to me. "The Crown and Dolphin should be our first port of call. There's always news to be had in a public house."

The atmosphere in the Crown and Dolphin was as nautical as one might have expected so near the Docks.

Mirrors lined the wall above the long bar, and the other walls were covered with prints of ships and sailors and hung with nautical paraphernalia. A festoon of holly branches above the fireplace was the Crown and Dolphin's single concession to the coming festive season.

A group of bearded men o' war's men in naval uniform sat or stood around a circular table in one corner supping beer and quietly watching five of their number play a dice game.

Another group, Maltese or Italian by their accents, stood at one end of the long bar babbling in their shrill tones and gesticulating wildly.

At the other end of the bar, the four women we had seen leaving the fortune-teller's house drank brown ale and chatted.

We sat at a small, round table near the door and ordered beers from a solemn Chinese boy who acted as waiter. He brought two pints of bitter ale to our table.

"Lot of fuss next door, by all accounts," Holmes said with an arch look.

The boy fixed Holmes with his blank almond eyes.

Holmes winked. "I hear that whoever or whatever's next door can tell the future. Is that right, sonny?"

The boy held his hand out for payment. I gave him fourpence and he walked away without a smile or thank you.

Holmes shrugged and sipped his beer.

Over his shoulder I saw the glass entrance doors swung wide open and a half dozen heavily built, bearded men in fur or sealskin coats and leather hats bustle in. They crowded around a table next to us, dragging stools, and then a second table into the alcove and piling their malodorous coats and hats on it. From the nautical tattoos they had on their arms and the strong reek they exuded, it was evident they were fishermen. They hooted and growled amiably at each other in a language I could not recognise, and they called for beer in guttural English.

Holmes took another sip of his beer and nodded towards the four women at the bar. "Women are your province, Watson; find out what they know about next door."

I refused to do anything of the sort, and we supped our beers in strained silence.

A short, stout man in a bowler, with a thick, black walrus moustache appeared before us. "Morning, gentlemen, I hope everything is to your satisfaction," he said, doffing his hat. "If you've a mind to eat, we have a fine roast and vegetables with all the trimmings for eightpence ha'penny."

"Good morning, Mr Latimer," Holmes said.

The man was taken aback.

"Your name is on the door lintel, if you are the landlord," I explained, earning a reproachful look from Holmes.

"I do not have that privilege, gentlemen. No, Mr Latimer had a seizure, and he has taken to his bed these last several months. Nevertheless, you won't find a better pint anywhere in Stepney, nor Wapping, neither. Always full measure at the Crown and Dolphin, sirs, and no hanky-panky with the foam, not in a house run by George Taylor – on Mr Latimer's behalf, naturally."

"Naturally," said Holmes. "We were drawn to this area by the fine reputation of your beer and by the strange tales we hear about next door."

Mr Taylor sniffed and lowered his voice. "Fuss and feathers is my opinion, sirs. Any fool could tell Ormande would win the Derby. I had ten bob on him myself with no fiddle-faddle of oracles in it. I rely on the Pink 'un." He pulled a copy of the *Sporting Times* from his pocket. "No fairies or disembodied voices here, sirs, just honest British sportsmanship and fair play for all. A nice roast is it, gentlemen?"

Holmes pushed away his almost untouched beer and stood. "Thank you, no, Mr Taylor, we have to be on our way. Perhaps we might—"

A man in a black sealskin coat with an enormous white moustache rose from the sailors' table and stared hard at Holmes. He raised his full glass in salute and grinned, his blackened teeth and deep-blue eyes gleaming in the lamplight.

Mr Taylor stood back against the wall and folded his arms as the pub went needle-dropping quiet.

"Cheers!" the man cried in strongly accented English.

Holmes shrugged on his overcoat, wrapped his scarf around his neck and set his top hat on his head.

I tensed and readied my walking stick under the table as Holmes reached for his beer glass and lifted it in salute, "*Gezondheid Kapitein!*"

"*Proost!*" the man shouted, and Holmes and he drained their beers in long swallows.

The man's companions roared their approval, thumping on the table, before they obliged me to go through the same ritual.

I endured manly claps on the shoulders and back from the friendly sailors before I staggered out of the public house behind Holmes.

We picked our way along the icy pavement, through drifts of filthy slush, past the Oracle's lair to the entrance of the carnival show next door.

The house was a grim, two-story building with double the frontage of the dwelling next door. The windows on either side of the central door were entirely covered with layers of lurid posters advertising the displays inside.

The show was, I suppose, typical of its kind. One poster depicted a maniacal-looking man, drenched in blood, brandishing a massive blood-stained hammer, and another promised a life-sized wax recreation of the death of General Gordon at Khartoum in the previous year, with hourly live tableaux.

We pushed through the curtain into a small lobby. The walls were plastered with posters even more garish and indeed lewder than the ones outside. Scantily dressed women cowered before brutes with knives or arched backwards as stranglers' hands enveloped their throats.

"I say, Holmes, this is atrocious."

A heavily made-up young woman sat at a desk in front of a curtained doorway. "Penny each, gents," she said. "And we ain't got no change, so it's no use asking."

"We wish to meet the proprietor," said Holmes.

The girl looked blankly at him.

"The boss," he explained.

She opened a drawer below the desk, took out a small brass bell and rang it.

The curtain parted, and a huge, shaven-headed man pushed through and stared suspiciously at us through one eye; the other was a wrinkled socket. His misshapen hands were balled into fists.

"What's the to-do?" he asked. "Jacks, is it?"

The curtain parted again, and a thin, cadaverous man edged past him and held out his hand.

"Albert Pargeter at your service, gentlemen," he said in a cultured tone and with a slight lisp.

"I am Sherlock Holmes."

"A privilege to meet you at last, Mr Holmes. Do come in."

Mr Pargeter led Holmes and me past the bruiser, through the curtain and into a large, low-ceilinged room with a stage at the far end.

A group of men blacked up as natives and carrying spears lounged on stage, smoking. Behind them a wax effigy of a fair-haired, stern-looking man in Army uniform sat on a camel. Along the side walls of the auditorium were curtained booths hung with posters advertising the ghastly crimes that were recreated in waxwork within. There were no customers.

"You see what I'm reduced to, gentlemen," Mr Pargeter said in a sad tone after Holmes had introduced me. "Gordon of Khartoum – one step up from the Death of Nelson and Kiss me, Hardy."

He shook his head as he contemplated the group on stage. "Mr Barnum and Mr Bailey in America exhibit Jumbo the elephant and the smallest person in the world, the Marvellous Mexican Midget Miss Zarate, just twenty inches high, and I subsist with Gordon and the mad Mahdi."

He waved a languid hand at the low, peeling ceiling above us. "I had hoped for a special appearance by Blondin, the aerialist, but after viewing the premises, he refused to countenance the engagement. I booked Chang, the Chinese Giant, but I was obliged to show him seated, which reduced the effect."

As Mr Pargeter spoke, I concentrated my gaze on the tableau on stage. On closer inspection, I could see that amongst the sham Sudanese warriors were maidens of the tribe in scanty attire.

"Monstrous," I murmured.

"Indeed so, Doctor," Mr Pargeter said with another long sigh. "We are enduring the worst run-up to Christmas in living memory, sirs, what with the fogs, freezing weather and all this talk of war with Russia."

He blinked at Holmes. "And it's not been a good year for murder, if you'll pardon the liberty."

Holmes raised his eyebrows. "There was the Camberwell Poisoning, and the Pimlico Mystery. Neither was entirely devoid of interest. And the Sanderson case has branched in unexpected directions."

"Oh yes, sir, the trade recognised what I hope I might call without undue familiarity your 'paw prints' in those cases."

Holmes smiled and bowed.

"Adelaide, the wife in the Pimlico matter was a comely defendant," Mr Pargeter continued, "and her looks weighed heavily with the jury, but poisoning, sir—"

He spread his hands. "You'll forgive me I'm sure when I say what the punters wants is blood – buckets of blood. No, Pimlico did not build a following, and the acquittal, although providential for the lady in question, did not excite my patrons in the way a hanging, a female hanging, would have."

"The pathologist in the Pimlico case was Sir James Paget," Holmes said. "He remarked to me that since the wife had been acquitted and she could not be tried again, she should, in all fairness, tell us how she committed the crime."

He took a cigar from his cigar case and gestured to a poster of a man with a bloody hammer above a booth on the right. "I see you have Harmer."

"Harmer the Hammerer, as was topped last week, but after him, what?" Mr Pargeter shook his head. "We can't keep showing repeats, though I have to admit the Penge beheading still brings them in. No, what the public want are new murders and assassinations, and the more macabre the better."

"What of the disembodied voice? The Ratcliffe Oracle. Has that not increased your business?" I asked.

Mr Pargeter considered. "We've had one or two foreign tourists pop in after they have experienced the phenomenon. Not a big draw though; spectral sounds are all very well, but what the punters want is—"

"Blood," Holmes said with a genial smile.

I left Holmes chatting with Mr Pargeter, and I wandered across the room to the stage to inspect the tableau of General Gordon.

I regarded the display with pursed lips. The general's camel was obviously stuffed, for it had lost one of its legs and it leaned against a hat stand.

The ladies playing Sudanese maidens were in outrageously revealing costumes. One young girl bent across the footlights towards me, displaying portions of her bosom where the black make-up had not been applied that were quite pearly white. She requested a cigarette, and I passed her one from my packet and lit it with a match.

I smoothed my moustache and looked for a way onto the stage so I might remonstrate with her at closer quarters and persuade her to cover herself in more modest raiment. I thought—

"Watson?"

"I'm just—"

"Come along, my dear fellow. There is no time to be lost," said Holmes.

I knew it was no use arguing with Holmes, and as I trudged back to the entrance, I reflected that my friend's single-minded pursuit of criminals might be better tempered by more concern for the moral reform of members of the unfortunate classes. He might find an example in our great statesman, Mr Gladstone, who nightly prowled the streets around Parliament accosting ladies of the night and offering hot baths and the solace of scripture.

Holmes shook hands with Mr Pargeter. "Good day to you, sir. Let's hope for both our sakes the murder and mayhem artists in the capital shake off their injurious lethargy in the New Year."

I said goodbye and followed Holmes through the lobby and into the street.

"The carnival gentleman seemed pleased with your acquaintance, Holmes," I said as we stood outside the theatre and buttoned our gloves. "How did he know who you were?"

"I am tolerably well known, at least by reputation, in those circles whose business takes them to the police courts. He is cheered because I informed him of the Montrouge murders. A telegram yesterday from Inspector Dubougue of the Sûreté requested I review the facts of the case.

"A female torso was deposited on the steps of Montrouge church in Paris. It is a fresh murder, and I doubt news has reached the British press. Mr Pargeter will have a scoop. The head, legs and arms of the victim had been removed and are missing. The killer excised other parts of the victim's anatomy: her right—"

"I say, Holmes!"

Holmes threw his scarf around his neck and over his shoulder. "Mr Pargeter was captivated; I have promised to send him full details and autopsy photographs."

"What now?" I eyed the welcoming windows of the Crown and Dolphin. "Lunch? Oh, how did you know those sailors were German?"

"Dutch, in fact. I assessed their clothes, deportment, accents and there were olfactory clues—"

"The fishy stink?"

"—the fishy stink, that convinced me they were the crew of a Dutch eel boat. They deferred to the fellow with the enormous moustache, so he was evidently their *kapitein*."

Holmes shrugged. "They spoke in Dutch. Hollands is instantly recognisable as a defrocked or fractured German by the harshness and the peculiarity of the tone."

He took my arm. "Come, let's meet the Voice."

I sighed and walked with Holmes to the house next door to the Carnival. The queue had vanished.

Holmes tapped on the door with his stick. We waited, and nothing happened. He tapped again.

The door opened an inch, and we saw an eye. "We're closed for dinner, twelve to one – oh, proper gentlemen."

The door opened wide and the thin man in the long overcoat and threadbare bowler we had seen earlier stood aside to let us in.

The chill, shabby hall was lit by a single, dim oil lamp and the walls were draped with black cloth. A plaster bust of Napoleon standing on a waist-high plinth was its only decoration. A strong smell of incense pervaded the gloomy atmosphere.

"The phenomenon can be experienced anywhere in the house, sirs, but the room above is its favourite, like," the custodian said. "We had Mr Stead from the *Pall Mall Gazette* in here last week and that Mr Oscar Wilde and his lady wife."

He led us up the dark stairs to the top of the house and opened the door of what had been a bedroom. The windows were heavily curtained, and the room was lit only by a shaded oil lamp.

A plain, square table with four chairs stood on the bare floorboards. A bowl of incense sat on a small brazier in front of a brick fireplace and chimney. No fire was lit in the grate, and the atmosphere was dank and chilly.

"We let people in by fours, gents," the man explained. "They sit, hold hands and call for the spirit. That usually brings her."

He motioned us to seats on opposite sides of the table. "If you would take the other gentleman's hand, sirs," he suggested.

I coloured. "I will do nothing of the sort."

"Well, sir, I cannot guarantee the phenomena will make itself known to you, without you hold hands. Was there any particular spirit you wanted to make a connection with, a relative passed over perhaps, or is it a general question?"

He stepped back to the wall behind the chimney breast and leaned against it.

I ignored him, took a cigar from my case and busied myself cutting and lighting it.

There was a long silence, with just the sound of the icy wind whistling down the chimney.

Holmes stood. "I believe you are right, young man. The spirit is offended at my friend's boorish refusal to—"

A long, low moan and a sepulchral voice, somehow neither male nor female and uttering words and phrases just on the edge of understanding, filled the room. It seemed to steady and become more coherent. "What?" it asked in a peremptory tone.

"You can ask the apparition your question now, gents," the custodian said. "One each is the rule."

Holmes smiled at me.

"Um, I was wondering when, that is, ah how—"

"My friend is wondering when he might find a suitable young lady for the purpose of marriage," said Holmes.

"I say, Holmes. I was going to ask about Blackheath Rugby Club's chances next Saturday; it's the key game of the season!"

"September!" cried the voice, and there was another long silence.

"I'm afraid that's it, gents. I'm surprised the apparition was so polite as to manifest, what with you not creating the circle, like."

"Why don't you go and have your dinner," Holmes suggested. "We'll wait here quietly to see if the phenomenon reoccurs. My friend is too shy to hold hands in company, but I might persuade him if we were alone."

I drew myself up. "I will do nothing of the sort, Holmes."

"I'm not supposed to—" the custodian began.

Holmes smiled. "We are happy to pay a half-crown and as much again when you return."

He nodded to me, and I produced a half-crown from my waistcoat pocket and flicked it to the man, who caught the coin and smiled broadly.

"There's no charge for the séance, but a tip is always welcome as your true gentleman knows. That Mr Wilde gave me a half-sovereign and his address, if I'd care to call."

The custodian opened the door. "I was about to pop next door to the Crown and Dolphin for seafood pie when you knocked. They do a memorable seafood pie, gents. Won't be two shakes, then I'll give you a private tour of the premises."

The door closed behind him, and Holmes gripped my arm. "Sound the walls, old chap; use your cane."

He turned the oil lamp up to its brightest setting, whipped out his magnifying glass and lay full length on the floor, examining the floorboards and the cracks between them. I moved along the walls, tapping first at the skirting board then farther up the walls. The walls sounded solid enough. The brickwork above the chimney was hollow of course, but I could find nothing of interest in the fabric of the room.

I leaned back against the wall by the chimney breast and relit my cigar. In the flare of the match, I noticed in the corner a thin wire that ran from the floor to the ceiling. "Holmes."

He and I examined the wire. "It looks like a bell wire," I suggested. Holmes pulled it, and the wire moved easily for a few inches, like a bell-pull, but there was no sound.

"Interesting," said Holmes. "You have your stethoscope, Watson?"

I took off my top hat, extracted the stethoscope and passed it to him. Holmes put in the earpieces and pressed the bell of the device to the wall.

I started as the low moaning sound again filled the room. There was a long hiss and a gabble of voices, then another moan was followed by a shrill, high voice with a slight Oriental accent. "What do you seek?"

Holmes gestured for me to answer as he moved along the wall and chimney breast listening.

"Um, I was wondering, ah, about the Club's next fixture. It's Blackheath versus—"

The door opened, and the custodian peeked in, blinked at Holmes and burst out laughing. "I heard the spectre manifest. You reporters or jacks?"

"Neither," I answered shamefacedly. "We are merely interested in the phenomenon."

"We had a Scotch doctor from Southsea in here last month sounding the floorboards, and a pair of jacks from Scotland Yard turned up after clues to the Sanderson affair."

There were no further ghostly sounds, and the custodian saw us to the front door.

"What time do you close?" Holmes asked him.

"The manifestation beds down for the night at ten, sir."

"You live here?"

"Oh, no, sir. I have a room at the Crown and Dolphin."

"You mentioned Scotland Yard detectives enquired about the Sanderson case," Holmes said to the custodian as we followed him downstairs and outside. "Did the spectral voice have anything to say on the matter?"

"She said it was the lodger."

Holmes sniffed. "Ha, the lodger indeed."

The snow had started again, and the pavement was covered with a thin layer of snow over ice and slush, but, despite the weather, a queue of people, mostly women, waited outside the door. The custodian ushered four of them inside.

Holmes drew his scarf around his neck and grinned. "Lunch: what do you say to the roast at the Crown and Dolphin?"

"A capital suggestion."

A boy of nine or ten marched up to us and brought a long broom to the salute. Holmes returned the salute and pointed up the road. The boy walked before us sweeping the pavement clear until we stopped outside the door of the public house.

"Give the boy a ha'penny, Watson."

The boy looked up, scowled and brushed snow over my boots.

"A penny," Holmes said, beaming at the boy. "You will go far, young man. You show a fine enterprising spirit. How would you like to earn thruppence?"

The boy nodded warily, and he listened as Holmes murmured in his ear. He held out his hand.

"Give the fellow tuppence, Watson, the balance payable in the Crown and Dolphin when he returns with the article."

THE RATCLIFFE HIGHWAY AFFAIR · 75

"What article, Holmes?" I asked as I handed the boy two pennies.

Holmes pushed through the heavy glass doors into the warm fug of the public bar of the Crown and Dolphin. It was, I was glad to see, empty of Dutchmen, although the Navy, the Maltese, and the four women were still there. We returned to our table by the windows and ordered beers and the daily roast from the Chinese boy.

"Well, Holmes? What have you discovered?"

He nodded at the group of four women who were still at the bar. They were collecting their things and moving towards the door.

I turned and followed his gaze. "Good Lord, Holmes, our maid is with them."

I made to stand, but Holmes took my arm and smiled at someone behind me. The young street sweeper came to our table with a wizened, middle-aged man in a grimy suit.

"Give the boy tuppence, Watson. I believe he has brought us a genuine nuller."

I paid the boy and received a grin and another salute with his brush as he turned away. Holmes gestured for the man to sit and bade me order him a pint of beer.

"Your name?" Holmes asked.

"Larkin, sir, James Larkin," said the man.

The solemn Chinese boy placed a beer in front of Mr Larkin, who took a gulp and smiled. "If it's top-class chimney sweeping you want done, sirs," he said, "you have come to the right man."

Holmes leaned across the table and murmured. "I'm looking for a climbing boy."

The sweep tapped his finger to the side of his nose. "Illegal, that is, gents. No climbing boys is allowed any more by act of Parliament."

He straightened and hooked his thumbs behind his lapels. "I've been on the sweep these fourteen years, gents, starting as a 'prentice. I shinned up many a chimney when I was a nipper and I still have the calluses on me elbows and knees to prove it. It was a fine life for a lad: hard, but with prospects. Then that Lord Shaftsbury poked his nose in, and boys was banned. I'll tell you, sir, us ex-sweeps boys burn a guy every Guy Fawkes Day, but ours ain't Mr Fawkes at all, it's bleedin' faint-heart Lord Shaftsbury."

He took an emphatic slurp of beer. "I muddled through somehow and set myself up in me own business. I don't know as I'm what you'd call a nuller, a top master of the sweeping craft, but I'm my own man with nothing owed to no bugger, pardon my French. I provide the professional service the nobs require, but, there ain't no climbing boys to be had, sir, not for—"

Holmes placed his hand on the table and briefly uncovered a gold half-sovereign.

Larkin smiled. "I can see you are a man who demands the best, sir. You know there's no substitute for a human brush. The big houses up West have chimneys branching all over and they're deathly afraid of chimney fires; deathly afraid are the Quality."

He took another long slurp of beer, wiped his mouth with his sleeve and glared around the room before he continued. "Your proper chimney boy, your well-trained and nimble lad, can get into every crevice see, into where the pole brushes can't get; why? 'Cos the poles don't bend easy is why. Your supple lad can squeeze in and get out all the soot. He can scrape off the black muck as catches fire and set all clean and safe. How big's the flue?"

Holmes waved his question away. "We will meet here tonight at ten pm exactly. Watson, give Mr Larkin two half-crowns as a deposit."

I counted out the money, and Larkin swept the coins off the table.

"You will receive a further five shillings when the job is done," said Holmes. "Agreed?"

The sweep nodded, stood, wiped his hand on his jacket and held it out. Holmes ignored the gesture and waved him away just as the Chinese boy arrived with two steaming plates of roast beef with, as the Americans say, all the trimmings.

Our maid, Bessie, stood white-faced before Holmes in our sitting room.

"What were you doing in Cable Street, Bessie?" I asked gently.

"Which I was sent to Whiteley's by Mrs Hudson to collect the Christmas bunting what was ordered special, and she says as how I could take an hour or so to visit my mum that lives in Pennington Street just across from the Highway."

"And you visited the Oracle," said Holmes. "Relate your experience."

She looked blankly at him.

"Tell us about the Voice," I said.

Bessie sighed a long sigh. "It's my Ernie, my younger brother as was. He died of consumption a year ago aged just nine, sir, and the cutest, bonniest – oh, Doctor."

"There, there, my dear." I helped Bessie to a seat at our supper table and fetched her a glass of brandy, ignoring Holmes' 'tuts' and impatient mumbles. "Now, Bessie, was the apparition you heard—"

"It cannot be an apparition if we don't see it," Holmes snapped. "Let us at least get our terms right."

I sighed. "Tell us about the Voice, Bessie."

"It was lovely, Doctor," she said, her bright eyes glistening. "Little Ernie is content in Heaven – a special children's Heaven with toys and everything. He's eating well, too."

"Great grief," Holmes muttered.

"And the other ladies?" I asked. "The ones with you – were they also happy with the Voice's messages?"

"Oh, yes, sir. One lady, the one in the green mantle, the silky one, goes every day to talk with her daughter, Emily, what was knocked down by a dray in Moncrieff Street down Peckham way."

"Cost?" Holmes asked.

"No charge," Bessie said, pouting. "But you can leave thruppence tip for Henry. I can't go every week, not on my wages."

Holmes waved her away. "Coffee, and the evening papers."

"No fee," I said as the door closed behind our maid. "That's strange. Even at thruppence for a consultation, with four customers every fifteen minutes it comes to an amount not to be sniffed at."

"Three paying customers, Watson. The green-shawled lady is a shill. She, and perhaps others, draw in the punters with silky tales of daughters and Peckham drays."

"Still," I said. "With a half-crown or more in tips now and then from the gentry, it must rake in a pretty penny. If I had that income from my medical practice, I would not be unsatisfied."

"Quack religiosity pays, my dear fellow. Man, or in this case woman is infinitely gullible. But fortune-telling for profit, however common it may be, is against the law. The tip is to view the Oracle's lair. It is a cunning ruse and a clever hoax."

"You are certain it is a hoax?" I asked.

"Ha! Not just a hoax, my dear fellow, a criminal conspiracy of the darkest, most ruthless hue."

We took a cab to Cable Street that evening through wisps of grey fog that obscured the full moon.

We stopped once more at the Crown and Dolphin and pushed through the heavy door into the public bar.

The room was busy with dock workers and sailors, mostly standing at the bar. The smell of the commodities the men had been loading or storing – tobacco, tar, spices, hides and fish created a stench of Jamrachian intensity.

Holmes led me to a corner table. "We will only have time for halves."

The master sweep appeared at the back door of the pub as our drinks were delivered. He was trailed by a young boy in ragged, grimy clothes. I recognised him immediately.

"Holmes," I said. "It's the impertinent pup from this morning: the street sweeper."

Larkin and the boy slipped into seats beside us. The boy winked at me.

"All right young fellow, what's your name?" Holmes asked.

"Finn, sir," the boy answered.

"Very good Master Finn, now I want—"

"Just Finn, sir. Mr Larkin's my master."

"Finn. I want you to climb up inside a chimney and look around. You don't have to sweep, just inspect the flue."

The boy gave Holmes a suspicious look. "What's up there, then?"

"I don't know, that's why – Watson!"

Larkin and the boy rose from their seats and made to leave.

I stood. "What Mr Holmes is saying is there may be something unusual inside the chimney. Nothing dangerous, mind. Just out-of-place, like a, like a – like a what exactly, Holmes?"

"Like a pot of gold, or a sovereign each."

Slow smiles spread over the faces of the sweep and his apprentice, and they sat.

Behind them, the street door opened and the young man from the house of the oracle came in, and behind him was a familiar figure. They pushed through the crowd to the bar.

"I say, Holmes, look who—"

"We must be off," he overrode me, checking his watch. He stood. "But first—" He strode to the bar, disappearing in the crowd. The sweep and his boy frowned at me, and I looked blankly back.

A moment later Holmes reappeared, swept his hat from the table and led us outside.

"I'll get my brushes," the sweep said as we stood on the pavement under a large gas lamp. "They're in a lock-up just—"

"No need," Holmes ushered us next door, to the house of the Oracle. He unlocked the door and led us in, locking the door behind us. I lit my dark lantern.

Finn looked fearfully up at Holmes. "This is where the ghost lives."

"Nonsense," Holmes said, planting his top hat on the marble head of Napoleon. "Give the boy a sweetie, Watson."

We followed Holmes upstairs to the room he and I had examined previously.

He lit the oil lamp. "Remove that stinking brazier, would you? Put it outside, old chap."

I gingerly picked up the incense brazier from the fireplace and stood it in the hall.

I returned to the bedroom, closed the door and leant against it as Holmes drew back several layers of black curtain material from the window, and moonlight streamed into the room.

He nodded to Finn, and the boy pulled off his shoes and jacket, jammed on his leather cap, and slid face up into the fireplace.

He lay for a moment staring up into the flue. "No moonlight, gents. She's blocked, or mebbe she branches off."

He stood, and we could see only his legs, then he was gone, and a steady dribble of soot fell onto the empty grate. The sweep produced a canvas bag from his coat pocket, knelt and swept the soot into the bag. "Worth a bit, soot; they make ink from it."

"I must say, Holmes," I said, "I'm uncomfortable with our situation. Employing a climbing boy to sweep a chimney is illegal. A policeman could take us in charge without a warrant."

"He is not sweeping the flue, he is investigating it."

"And what about unlawful entry and trespass?" I whispered. "I know perfectly well who dipped the key from the custodian of the oracle; he was in the public house with him."

Holmes winked.

A huge fall of soot spilled from the grate and billowed across the room, and I turned away and covered my nose with my handkerchief. The sweep continued to fill his bag, humming contentedly to himself.

The soot settled, and Holmes offered me his cigar case. "We are both somewhat spotted, a little cigar ash won't matter."

A further fall of ash and soot was followed by a scrabbling noise from the grate, and a pair of legs appeared in the fireplace. The sweep helped the boy out. He was black from head to toe and shivering. He spoke quietly to the sweep as he shook his hair and brushed his trousers over the soot bag.

They stood.

"Well, sirs," said the sweep. "Finn says there's no pot of gold nor anything else up that flue. He says it ain't been lit this age; the chimney was clear for fifteen feet or so, then blocked solid with soot, birds' nest, leaves and other stuff that fell through from above."

"Nothing else?" asked Holmes.

Finn shook his head, depositing more soot onto the floor.

Holmes brushed at his clothes with his handkerchief. "I had expected – well, never mind. One hypothesis is scotched; we must move on."

"That'll be a guinea each, sir," said Larkin. "What with it was a custom job and what with the law—"

"Yes, yes," Holmes said, reaching for his scarf and stick. "Pay the man, Watson, and a bob, no two-bob tip for Finn."

The boy grinned and then frowned. "You don't mean the hole, do you, sir?"

Holmes spun and faced the boy, his eyes sparkling. "You saw a hole? Describe, no, better yet, let me have your notebook, Watson. The boy can draw his hole."

"I say, Holmes." I reluctantly took my notebook from my inside pocket and laid it on the table.

The boy jumped several times, whacking his arms together to warm himself and creating a cloud of soot that billowed from him and settled over us. I handed him my pencil, and he licked the end and considered the notebook page. After several moments' thought he drew a neat circle and handed back my pencil.

I laughed.

"No, no, Watson. Young Finn has drawn a perfectly round hole. It cannot be natural. It is not a crack or crevice; it is man-made. That is of the first importance."

Finn grinned at my discomfiture and blinked up at Holmes.

"The location of this hole, young man," Holmes asked. "Where is it, exactly? I must have precise data."

The boy described how he had climbed, feet, back and elbows braced against the inside of the chimney for twelve or fifteen feet. The flue was clean and mostly clear of soot. He reached a blockage and jabbed at it with his elbow; the debris was dislodged and fell over and past him. He looked up and saw moonlight. The chimney was clear to the top.

Holmes sat still during the boy's narrative, his elbows bent, fingers steepled under his chin and eyes closed.

Finn said as he moved down, always the dangerous part of the job, he noticed a round hole in the wall like the mouth of a drainpipe.

"On your right or left," Holmes asked, leaning forward, his eyes bright and glittering.

"Straight ahead, sir."

"Ha!" Holmes exclaimed. "Ha, ha. The size of this hole, Finn–show!"

The boy curved his hands around an imaginary pipe six inches or so in diameter.

"And being a curious young man, you peered inside," Holmes said.

"Didn't see nothing, sir."

"And you felt around the lip of the pipe with your hand. Your left hand."

The boy's eyes widened. "I did, sir, to—"

"To test what it was made of."

"I'm sorry, sir," said Larkin. He made to cuff the boy. "Finn always was a curiosity."

"No, no," Holmes said, "let him be." He smiled down at the boy. "And what did you discover?"

Finn shrugged. "The pipe is main clean, no soot or mess at all. It's smooth, not like clay and not lead."

"Pottery? Glazed pottery?" asked Holmes.

The boy shook his head. "Too thin. And it narrowed." He put his hands together in a vase shape.

"A cone?"

"The boy looked confused.

"Like a sugarloaf at the grocer's," I suggested, handing him another humbug. I held up the packet. "Or a pack of sweets wrapped in paper with a twist, narrow at the bottom and wide at the top."

He nodded. "I know what it felt like," he said, popping the sweet into his mouth. He pulled a folding clasp knife with a shiny brown handle out of his pocket and handed it to Holmes.

Holmes passed it to me.

"Bone-handled," I said, handing the knife back to the boy.

Holmes sat at the table, beamed at us and consulted his watch. "They will be starting their late supper orders. Yes, I think we might cause a little mayhem."

He looked up at me. "A cone made of horn, Watson. What does that bring to mind?"

"Horn? Drinking horns, knife handles, fog horns—"

"Exactly. If you blow into a horn, it makes a loud noise, and if you call through one, your voice is amplified. We are looking at a voice pipe or speaking tube. I made a detailed study of one I found embedded in a statue of Saint George in a church in Barcelona. I had hoped to publish a monograph on the subject, but I was chased away by a murderous mob led by the Bishop of *Sant Feliu de Llobregat*. I barely escaped with my life."

I blinked as I digested a rare moment of Holmes' personal history.

"And who is the culprit? Who installed this system of voice pipes?"

"I have an idea, but I am by no means certain. Anyway, I have exposed the Limehouse Sibyl; my work here is done."

I frowned. "But you must be interested in the reason for the deception. Who installed the device and to what purpose?"

"*Cui bono*, my dear fellow, who benefits? It is usually obvious and seldom worth a deal of thought."

"They don't charge for entrance or to question the Voice," I mused. "Is it an advertising device? Buy Burgess's Noted fish-sauce? Mr Pargeter might make much of his Gordon at Khartoum."

"He would hardly want to finance a rival attraction next door to his carnival," Holmes suggested. He grinned, picked up my pencil, wrote in my notebook, and turned to the boy.

"Now Finn, I want you to go back up the flue again and plant yourself opposite the hole. I want you to shout this message into the hole. Can you read?"

The boy shook his head and his face paled. "Talk to the ghost?"

Holmes snapped his fingers in impatience. "There is no ghost – bah!"

He leaned close to the boy. "It is a game, yes, a kind of prank. You will call out, and Watson and I will provide background noises of a ghoulish kind. Mr Larkin may second us, if he so chooses."

He whispered in Finn's ear. The boy nodded, grinned, pulled himself into the grate and disappeared up the chimney.

"Let me know when you are comfortable, my boy," Holmes called.

"All right."

"Ha, ha," Holmes cackled. "Watson, jerk on the bell wire. Jerk in random patterns."

"Revenge!" Finn called. The words echoed around the room. "Revenge! Toungoo! Toungoo!"

"Ooooh, aaaagh, wooo," cried Holmes in a ghostly tone. Larkin hallooed with him.

"Come along Watson," Holmes said sharply, "do show willing. Larkin is much ghoulier than you are."

Finn came tumbling down into the grate. "There's people in the hole! I heard their voices. They said they'd have my guts for garters."

"Give the boy another humbug," Holmes said, handing me a key. "Then he and Mr Larkin may care to leave us before our guests arrive."

I led the sweep and Finn downstairs and let them out into the street. I relocked the door and re-joined Holmes upstairs where he sat, smoking.

He pointed to the ceiling. "You will have noticed the Elizabethan beams. They are crosswise, not fore and aft. The Stuarts introduced new regulations after the Great Fire. The basic fabric of this row of houses is Elizabethan."

"And so?"

"Rooms were constructed by Elizabeth's spymasters into which they would lure suspected dissidents and encourage them to incriminate each other while the spies listened in. I believe Kit Marlowe—"

A thunderous banging came at the door downstairs, and I stood.

"Wait. The other party will have a spare key."

There was a rumble on the stairs, and Taylor and the custodian of the Voice slammed the door open and strode into the room. Taylor held a large calibre revolver.

"Ah, would you, now?" said a figure behind him. The revolver was knocked to the floor, and Taylor pushed against the wall. I picked up the gun and looked up into the face of Wiggins, the head of Holmes' band of street Arabs, the Baker Street Irregulars. He slapped a heavy life preserver in his gloved hands.

The temporary landlord of the Crown and Dolphin massaged his arm and surveyed the room.

"Well gentlemen, we shall have a talk," Taylor said. "Then I will summon a constable to arrest you for trespass and assault."

"And pickpocketing," said the custodian. "Someone dipped my front door key."

Holmes laughed.

"You think to take me in charge for the Voice?" Taylor said coolly. "I broke no laws – no fee was charged." He took a cigarette from a packet and lit it with a match.

"Mr Taylor, or shall I call you Thrope?" Holmes asked with a jaguar grin. "You and your minions are in my power. Your only chance for salvation is to tell me everything. From the beginning if you please."

The custodian lunged for the door, pushed past Wiggins and ran out. I jumped up and thundered down the stairs after him. The street door was open, and my quarry raced outside and pushed through a knot of people, mostly women, who waited outside.

I stood on tiptoe and looked over their heads. The man was visible in the bright moonlight, running hard. He turned left into Cable Street.

I elbowed through the crowd, ran to the corner and stood under a street lamp. He was nowhere in sight. He had evidently ducked into an alley. I walked along the pavement for a few yards and then, feeling foolish, I pocketed Taylor's revolver and returned to the house.

The crowd had disappeared, local people peeked out of their doorways, and the vendors outside the pub huddled together, staring at me.

I found only Holmes and Wiggins in the room upstairs.

"There you are, Watson," said Holmes. "You were very spry. Did you get him? No?"

Holmes held out his hand and Wiggins counted two shillings into his palm. "I gave you two to one," said Wiggins with a grin. "I thought you had a good chance."

"Never mind, my dear fellow," said Holmes. "Let's repair next door for refreshment."

I followed him down to the lobby where he retrieved his top hat from the Napoleon bust, and we stepped outside.

"How—" I began.

"Oh, it was simple enough. Taylor was my principal suspect from the start. Let me show you."

He sent Wiggins on ahead to the Crown and Dolphin, and led me to the building next door, the brightly lit carnival.

"There, you see, Watson? This building, on the right side of the Sibyl's lair, is separate. There is no party wall or other connection. Unless it ran underground (highly unlikely from an upper-floor room) the speaking tube could not connect with Mr Pargeter's establishment. Our quarry was in the building on the other side, the public house, which shares a party wall with the oracle."

A young boy ran up, saluting with his broom, and I recognised the grimy face of Finn, the climbing boy. He brushed a clear path through the slush to the doors of the Crown and Dolphin.

Holmes ushered him inside with us to where Wiggins sat at the bar. "Wiggins, I commend this lad to you. I suggest you enrol him in the Irregulars at standard rates."

He turned to me with a grin. "Supper for Wiggins and the boy, Watson. They do a fine roast, and we have heard good reports on their sea-pie. Service may be a little slow as the establishment is shorthanded."

Holmes and I took the stairs down to the gentlemen's lavatory in the basement for a much-needed wash and brush up.

"Did you notice the skull on the bar counter?" he asked me. "It is that of John Williams, the alleged Ratcliffe Highway murderer. He was buried at the crossroads outside the Crown and Dolphin pub in 1811 with a stake through his heart. His body was unearthed by the gas company digging a trench last August. They say he killed seven people from two families. You may stroke the skull for luck for a farthing."

Holmes led me upstairs and to a table by the window. Through a clear section of the etched glass we saw Taylor, the young man from the Sibyl's lair and two women fling bundles on to a cart and drive away at the canter.

The solemn Chinese boy appeared and took our drinks order.

"Well, Holmes?" I asked, raising an enquiring eyebrow.

"You will recall from the newspaper accounts that the only son of the Marquis of Rawley, an ensign with the Cavalry, went missing near Toungoo in Upper Burma three months ago. There has been no solid news of the boy since then, although rumours abound. His father suffered a fatal stroke when he heard his son was lost, leaving his distraught wife and her daughter-in-law, the ensign's wife, to cope alone. Here is the letter I received from Lady Edith Crampton yesterday morning."

He passed me a sheet of fine paper watermarked with a coat of arms, on which a note was written by someone either very ill or in an agitated state.

"The missing ensign's wife asks for your help, Holmes, on a matter of great delicacy. She says friends on whom she might have relied are powerless in the face of her mother-in-law's conviction she is speaking to her son through the agency of the Ratcliffe Oracle."

Holmes nodded. "Lady Edith married Lord Crampton barely a year ago. She is, of course, an American. Our aristocrats would accept no other nationality for their brides last season."

"Good lord, Holmes, she writes of an armed expedition to be fitted out with tropical equipment with the object of searching for Lord Crampton in the jungles in Upper Burma. Ten thousand pounds is offered for his safe return. A colossal sum, Holmes!"

"The wife's father is Mr Duval, a railway magnate from New York. The Voice, gaining the trust of the Marchioness, instructed her to transfer the money to the account of Mr Taylor, a person the entity said acted as its earthly agent. The cheque was to be delivered tomorrow."

"How did you know Taylor was not who he pretended to be?" I asked.

"The accent first: he tried to hide a Belfast accent. Ha! I literally wrote the book on accents; there was no fooling me. His dyed hair was obvious from smears on the inside rim of his bowler, visible when he doffed it. The pierced ears no longer held gold rings and the shamrock tattoo on his neck had been removed leaving an acid scar, but I had no doubt that our Mr Taylor was Thrope the wife strangler. He escaped from Mountjoy Prison in Dublin last year."

"We must inform the police, Holmes."

Holmes took a sip of beer. "I am no police nark. For me, the how is more important than the who. Let them do their own work, and I will do mine. Thrope's wife was by all accounts a noisy and unprepossessing shrew and no loss to the world."

I considered. "There's a jest about misan-thropes that is just beyond my reach. Holmes. Give me a moment."

The Chinese boy passed us with a tray on which were two plates piled high with steaming sea-pie and vegetables. He served Wiggins and Finn at the bar.

"I say, Holmes—"

Holmes called the boy over to us. "Could your kitchen manage another two servings of sea-pie, young man?"

The boy nodded and disappeared behind in the bar.

"What an inscrutable boy," I remarked.

"He was more loquacious playing a Burmese bandit through the voice tube."

I blinked at Holmes.

"Oh, yes, the principals in the fraud have escaped for now, but the minions believe they are safe. There is no proof of their involvement. Let's hope they can produce an adequate supper without their master's supervision."

"If they catch Thrope, Mr Pargeter will be pleased," I suggested. "A local topping."

I looked across to the bar where Finn and Wiggins were eating their sea-pie. "How did you know the lad explored the hole with his left hand?"

Holmes eyes gleamed in the gas light. "You saw he was right handed. If you were hanging by your elbows and knees halfway up a chimney which arm would you use to explore and which to hold you fast?"

I opened my notebook. "I shall entitle this 'The Case of the Ratcliffe Oracle'." I looked again at the young sweep's drawing of the pipe and grimaced at a nasty thumb mark he had left on the page.

"Nonsense, Watson," said Holmes, playing his irritating mind-reading game. "That thumb mark is an adornment; it is the boy's signature. The drawing is a genuine Finn. Can you doubt that a bright, or at least a sensational future lies ahead of him? Leave it a few decades and then you might contact Sotheby's and put the drawing to auction. By the way, you have a smut on your nose."

He smiled as I dabbed at it with my handkerchief.

"You are right, of course, we must telegraph to Lestrade," he said, glancing at his watch. "We have given the hare his law. I shall suggest he digs up the garden. I am not convinced that the landlord Mr Lassiter has taken to his bed, unless it is a flower bed."

Wiggins and Finn raised their glasses to us from the bar, and we returned the compliment.

"Lady Crampton mentioned a heavy fee in her letter." I said.

Holmes smiled again. "I have booked a table at Romano's for nine tomorrow evening."

A paperboy appeared at the door with the early afternoon editions. His board offered sensational developments in the Sanderson poisoning case. I bought an *Evening News* and scanned the front page.

"I say, Holmes, there has been an arrest."

Holmes raised his eyebrows.

"The lodger," I said with a grin.

"Exactly as I suspected," said Holmes. "Ah, here is our sea-pie."

THE DeGASCOIGNE MUMMY

I stepped out of our hansom onto the wet pavement outside our lodgings in Baker Street.

"Did we remember, Billy?" I asked Holmes.

"Mrs Hudson bought him a new suit at Whiteley's in our name."

A crowd of ragamuffin children singing several Christmas carols at once and producing a dreadful cacophony surrounded us before we could reach the door of 221b.

"Watch your pocketbook," Holmes said as he carved his way through them.

Mrs Hudson ushered us into the hall, and we peeled off layers of scarves, waterproofs and coats.

"Letter for you, Mr Holmes," Billy said, holding out a blue envelope. "Come by special messenger while you were out."

Holmes pushed past him and took the stairs up to our sitting room three at a time. Billy grinned and handed me the envelope, and I followed Holmes upstairs at a more sedate pace.

"Never again," said Holmes as I entered the sitting room. He took a cigarette from the box on the side table and lit it with a match. "Shopping expeditions are too great a trial. I am weary beyond words."

"It was just to Gamages Emporium in Holborn and back, Holmes, and it's only once or twice a year. I thought we did well. They will deliver our purchases nicely gift-wrapped later today, leaving us a full two weeks in hand. But we must look to the Christmas cards; they are a neglected heap under your desk again."

Holmes slumped into his armchair. "Do you like your present? What was it? Oh, yes, an Inverness cape."

"It is in a fine, strong tweed."

"Good. I'll get you a deerstalker in the same fabric for your birthday, and you may venture North incognito, clad like a native. What's in the letter?"

I made to hand him the envelope, but he waved it away. "Read, my dear fellow. I have no secrets from you."

I opened the envelope, read the note and raised my eyebrows.

"No, no, not more ghosts!" Holmes cried. "These ghoulish commissions are degrading to the point of – what are you holding?"

I waved a cheque in Holmes' face.

He grabbed at it, but I pulled it away. "It is on Coutts for twenty pounds. Lady deGascoigne, the widow of Sir Edmund deGascoigne of Egyptologist fame, offers a twenty-pound fee for a twenty-minute consultation. A pound a minute: a princely rate, Holmes. I doubt that Jenny Lind commanded such a rate."

He sniffed. "A private consulting detective, unlike a concert hall warbler, is paid in guineas, or not at all."

"Not at all, then," I said, offering to cast the cheque into the fireplace.

Holmes snatched the cheque and subjected it to close examination. He smiled. "Coutts; they are a reliable firm. What are we expected to do to gain this sum?"

I glanced at our mantel clock. "The lady will communicate the matter to you today. She must be on her way, she mentioned two-fifteen in her letter and it is ten-past. The case concerns a missing Egyptian mummy."

"Great grief," said Holmes, flinging the stub of his cigarette into the fire.

"Language, Mr Holmes," Mrs Hudson admonished him from the doorway. She watered the aspidistra that stood on the sideboard. "As I have had to remind you on occasion, there's no need for words of that sort in a civilised house, especially in the Holy Season."

Holmes threw up his hands and slumped into his chair as the doorbell rang.

"That may be Lady deGascoigne," I said. I sprang to the window. "Yes, a fine carriage is at the kerb."

I opened the sitting-room door and saluted Holmes. "I shall leave you to your consultation."

Holmes jumped up. "Watson, you cannot desert me! You cannot leave me alone to talk of mummies with Lady whatever-her-name-is—"

"Lady Elizabeth deGascoigne," said a stern female voice with a strong American twang from the doorway behind me. "And mummies, Mr Holmes, are a dreadful bore."

A tall woman stalked past me into the sitting room, then turned and held out her hand. Lady Gascoigne was in full mourning, even the magnificent flowery hat she wore slantwise across her head was jet black and adorned with tiny black orchids and birds. A black net veil almost hid her face, but from the features I could see, I formed the impression she must be young and beautiful. Even in mourning attire she was quite strikingly—

"Doctor?" Holmes said softly.

I came out of my reverie, reddened and took her hand. "Doctor John Watson, at your service, Madame."

Lady deGascoigne lifted her veil over her hat brim and smiled. She was quite lovely, with milk-white skin, bright blue eyes and a delicate mouth. Holmes waved her to a seat on the sofa.

She frowned and held out her hand. "Come, Mr Holmes, shake the lady's hand. I am neither fragile nor diseased, and I am wearing sanitised kid leather gloves from Jacques Doucet of Paris at eighteen dollars the pair."

Holmes smiled, rose from his seat and shook Lady Gascoigne's hand.

She settled herself on the sofa and began in a business-like tone. "Gentlemen, I am the widow of Sir Edmund deGascoigne, who, as you are doubtless aware, was well-known as a collector of ancient Egyptian art and artefacts, and frankly for not much else. We were married for six years.

You should also know from the get-go I do not give a plugged nickel for Egypt and all its antiquities. It was my late-husband's interest, or should I say obsession, egged on by Bowen, our butler. My husband died a week ago, and I gave the butler a month's notice on the day of the funeral."

"My deepest condolences, Madame," I said.

"Your butler did not give satisfaction?" Holmes asked.

Lady deGascoigne pulled off her grey leather gloves, laid them on the occasional table beside her, and smiled a cat-like smile. "Oh, as butlers go, Bowen was well enough. He performed his duties, at least when he wasn't off somewhere in Egypt with my husband hunting for ancient knick-knacks. I hardly saw Edmund these three years, gentlemen, and when I did, he was so sun-burnt I could not exhibit him in polite society. No, I blame Bowen."

Lady deGascoigne shook her head. "The man was ridiculously spoiled by Edmund. Can you believe he put the butler's son through an expensive preparatory school and then sent the boy to Harrow where Charlie, Edmund's son by his first wife, was educated?"

She shook her head. "A servant's son at Harrow! What cruelty, to put a child into such an invidious position, educated far above his station and given hopes of rising into Society that must inevitably be dashed. I put an instant stop to that nonsense."

I watched incredulously as Lady deGascoigne helped herself to a cigarette from our case on the table.

"Never mind Bowen," she said. "He's out the door in three weeks and soon forgotten. Do you have a light?"

Holmes lit her cigarette with a spill from the fire with more self-possession than I could have mustered. I gave Lady deGascoigne a frigid look she appeared not to notice.

"My husband's collection of mummies, jewellery and other Egyptian items was an extensive one," she continued. "It was also, as I discovered far too late, very valuable. Under normal circumstances, of course, it would have gone to my stepson, Charlie."

She took a practised puff on her cigarette. "You are men of the world, gentlemen, so I'll be frank with you. Charlie requires a firm hand. He is not the brightest star in the social firmament by any stretch of the imagination. In cold fact, he's a dullard and something of a buffoon. But he has me as a step-mother and that makes a difference; that makes a significant difference."

She blew a stream of smoke across the room. "To get on in this country, and to marry well, requires money (which we have in just about the necessary amounts if certain vulgar interpretations of my husband's will are voided) and either charm or an elevation in rank. With Charlie, charm isn't an option, and being a sir by courtesy is all very well, but not enough to attract the match I want. I may admit to you gentlemen that it's difficult to place even an attractive boy with a top-notch, well-heeled family, and Charlie is not only dim, he is graceless. A girl comes bolstered with a dowry which can tip the balance but looks or breeding are necessary for a boy."

Lady deGascoigne considered as she took a long puff of her cigarette. "One can discount brains and talent: they are of no consequence among the English aristocracy."

I raised my eyebrows and gave Holmes an incredulous look. He smiled back at me.

"It was my aim to get my husband an elevation to the top of the heap, to the people that run things: the peers. I wanted something more serious than a mere Sir Edmund deGascoigne, a title that puts me at the bottom of a steep social ladder. I angled for a baronetcy, or better yet a viscountcy, if those are the terms."

She flicked the cigarette butt into the fire. "When I married Edward, I expected him to climb the ladder to a dukedom on daddy's bank account; naïve, you may say, but I and my dear, dear, father back in New York had little understanding of the aristocratic regime prevailing here in England. We did not understand your mechanisms of social advancement."

Lady deGascoigne lowered her eyes. "My father is no longer with us. A slimy, no-good business partner cleaned him out. Dad was a fine person, but trusting, and he departed this world a broken man."

She leaned back, and I frowned as she crossed her legs in an outré manner.

"Gentlemen, it's an American habit to set a price on things; we like to keep things simple. The English talk endlessly about birth and breeding in a way that is just plain gobbledegook to a plain-speaking person with a pragmatic cast of mind like myself. It is as if your aristos were bred at a stud farm."

She shook her head in bemusement. "It was obvious that if I was to develop the deGascoigne line into a dynasty, I required Royal patronage; it struck me I might parlay Edmund's Egyptian collection into a serious leg up in the peerage league, so I suggested to my husband he should donate his Egyptian antiquities to the nation. That would make our name known in Palace circles and might even reach a royal ear."

Lady deGascoigne smiled a wan smile. "I freely admit I was blinded to the value of the collection by a prejudice against its source (who had ever heard of an Egyptian sculptor or painter making a stir at Sotheby's or Christie's?). And donating the mummies to the British Museum had the charming consequence of ridding the ballroom and west wing of our townhouse of junk, thereby freeing the rooms for events during the social Season."

She smiled again. "I tried to veer Edmund's collecting obsession toward coinage, gold coinage of the current era, but he was not immediately moved (again I blame Bowen)."

Lady deGascoigne picked an imaginary fleck of lint from her jacket sleeve and regarded Holmes and me with a demure expression on her face. "However, I have a persuasive nature and I had, if I may say so, a strong influence on my husband in certain areas. I needed time to work on him."

I watched wide-eyed as Lady deGascoigne patted her hair and smiled.

"Would you care for tea, or coffee?" Holmes asked.

Lady deGascoigne leaned towards him. "I'm tempted to shock your medical friend further by demanding a Bourbon with American ice, but tea would be fine, thank you."

I found Billy lolling downstairs in the hall, and I ordered tea.

"It seemed obvious the collection was the way forward," Lady deGascoigne continued as I sat down again. "Edmund came around at last, and a month ago he signed an agreement to donate the mummies and the Egyptian jewels to the British Museum. I expected the nation to be properly grateful and thought in a year or so a suitable honour would be conferred on my husband."

She leaned across the table again and patted Holmes on the knee. "I engaged an advertising firm in the City to make sure the gift received adequate publicity: refined and sensitive, Mr Holmes, but crystal clear in terms of who gave what to whom."

She pursed her lips. "This seemed a fine plan until Edmund upped and died; heart failure, they said. I have no doubt he strained his heart climbing over those goddamned pyramids in the Egyptian sun. Ah here is tea."

Mrs Hudson stood in the doorway wide-eyed and pale with shock.

Lady deGascoigne rose. "Leave the tray on the table there, my good woman. I'll pour."

She waved Holmes and me back to our seats and continued. "Well, it's obvious the deGascoigne widow won't rate anything from Her Majesty but an invite to a garden party, so I tried to wiggle out from under the contract with the Museum and get the collection back. The jewellery is not to my taste, you understand, it is composed of poorly cut stones in gimcrack settings and I will countenance nothing but diamonds or pearls next to my skin, but can you believe the Museum had the stuff valued for insurance purposes at no less than ten thousand: that's sterling, gentlemen, not dollars. One lump or two, Doctor?"

"One, thank you."

She handed me a cup of tea. "Despite my serious, my vehement remonstrance, they refuse to return the goods."

Lady deGascoigne sighed. "So, now I'm out an honour, the mummies, the money and a husband, and left with an expensive idiot son, almost of age. One lump or two, Mr Holmes?"

Holmes waved sugar away and took his cup. Lady deGascoigne poured her own tea and returned to her place on the sofa.

"Gentlemen, I said I don't want to talk of mummies, but I have to touch on a note I received a few days ago from Mr Clarence Darling, the head of the Egyptian Department of the British Museum. He had sent men over to make an inventory of the collection a few weeks before the contract was signed. That list was used for checking the delivery when it arrived at the Museum. He intimates in his letter I sent them a dud mummy; he says one of the mummy cases, catalogued at my home as containing a mummy, was empty when it was opened for inspection at the British Museum.

They are a mummy short, and they ask for explanations. It is intensely vexing, in the circumstances."

Lady deGascoigne took a small pocket watch from her reticule and checked it against our mantel clock. "There now, Mr Holmes and Doctor Watson, I have laid my problem fairly before you in just over half my appointed time. Will you undertake to find the missing mummy? The fee for a successful conclusion to the matter is a hundred pounds."

She stood, picked up her gloves, and checked herself. "Oh, I am sorry gentlemen, a hundred guineas, of course." She looked from Holmes to me, "Each."

"Ha!" Holmes jumped to his feet and shook Her Ladyship's proffered hand. "I would be happy to resolve the mystery for you, Madame."

"Good. Mr Darling of the Egyptian Department is expecting you at the Montague Place entrance to the Museum this evening at five. Don't be late as he has another appointment for later. I had him dogged for the last week by another detective fellow, a Mr Barker, perhaps you know him?"

"My rival across the river," Holmes answered with a frown.

Lady deGascoigne smiled another demure smile. "Mr Barker discovered that on Friday evenings Mr Darling frequents Madame Lulu's establishment in the Haymarket. He likes to get there early enough to pick the best of the girls. His favourite is Florrie, and she is often taken off before he arrives."

I gaped at Lady deGascoigne like a guppy until Holmes poked me in the ribs to remind me of my manners and he and I accompanied Lady deGascoigne outside.

"Did you have me dogged, Madame?" Holmes murmured as he handed her into her carriage.

"Naturally, Mr Holmes, but I have discovered no skeletons in your closet, sir, nor any floozies; you are a man of mystery, an enigma, and therefore all the more alluring."

"Why did you not engage Mr Barker in the case?"

"He is competent," Lady deGascoigne replied with a smile, "but he is, after all, rather low. Ha! Coming from an American, that's amusing, *n'est-ce pas?*"

"What a dreadful person, Holmes," I said as Holmes and I returned to our sitting room. "Could you believe the cigarette? And that appalling calumny against an official of the British Museum!"

"Delightfully dreadful," Holmes said. "Pass me down the G index, would you?"

I took the relevant index down from the shelf above Holmes' desk and handed it to him. I pulled down a second volume, and we both leafed through our respective scrapbooks.

"No, nothing of Gascoigne," said Holmes. "Anything under deGascoigne?"

"Nothing."

"Then we shall have to consult our authority. It is nearly three. I have one or two little things to do, then we must to clubland, to St James's."

Holmes' college friend Langdale Pike sat at a small round table in his usual place in the bay window of his club in St James's Street. He wore a scarlet smoking jacket and fez, and a thick, black, knitted shawl lay across his shoulders.

Pike was the absolute authority on Society. His columns (weekly during the Season) kept the inquisitive informed on who was at the top of the heap and who was not. He knew whose reception had been attended by the Prince of Wales and, more piquantly, whose assemblies he had snubbed. Pike's delicate fingers lay on the harp strings of social position. He felt the slightest tremor in fashion, he foretold who would move up or down the social scale and he was alert to the faintest quiver of scandal.

His articles were read upstairs in the morning room over breakfast by Her Ladyship and even more eagerly downstairs in the servants' pantry by the butler and housekeeper that afternoon. By the end of the week, servants down to under-gardeners and boot boys had taken a position on every social question and acquired firm favourites among the Season's glamorous young debutantes.

"My dear fellow," Pike exclaimed as he saw Holmes. "I have been expecting you. And Doctor Watson too. I am overwhelmed, friends, to see you in such good health. Do sit down, my dear, dear chaps and let me order tea. They keep a special brew just for me. I get the leaves from a fellow who was in the India Service in Ceylon. He has a little man upcountry somewhere near Kandy who plucks each leaf individually for him. And the Club offers buttered toast of the highest quality."

Holmes took a seat beside his friend. "How are you, Pike?"

"Well, as far as one can be so in this dreadful weather, out of the Season and in this appallingly crass time of Christian jollity. The Club keeps my little cubbyhole free of Christmas detritus, but I have to pass that ridiculous tree in the lobby as I enter and exit. I avert my eyes; it is a stain on the Palladian aesthetic of the building. A German innovation, of course. Prince Albert has a lot to answer for, quite apart from his own frightful memorial."

Pike leaned forward. "It's the Amersham affair that brings you to me. Yes, yes, I have no doubt at all, Holmes; it is a pretty little mystery."

Holmes shook his head.

Pike picked up a slim notebook from the table and flicked through it. "But that is the only matter of consequence I have brewing at the moment." He blinked sorrowfully at Holmes.

"I had a visit from Lady Elizabeth deGascoigne this afternoon," Holmes said.

"Really? And what did Betsy Belle want of you?"

Holmes explained the circumstances of the lady's visit as an elderly waiter served tea and excellent buttered toast.

"She wants you to find a missing mummy?" Pike mused. "That's rich given her loathing of Egypt and all its works."

I sniffed. "She is an American, and a lady of a certain sort."

Pike stirred his tea. "Following the current fashion, Sir Edmund deGascoigne remarried into American money, and one must admit American beauty six or seven years ago. He needed an injection of cash as his gas mantle business was not flourishing. He had neglected his enterprise and spent far too much on his hobby."

"Mummies," I suggested.

"All sorts of Egyptian antiquities, including, as you say, one of the largest private collections of mummies in the country. His new wife tried to put a curb on his extravagance and had her husband employ a manager.

"From all accounts, the concern is back on its feet. And now Sir Edmund has passed over, leaving everything to son Charlie on his majority apart from one significant and extraordinary bequest."

"What of Lady deGascoigne's origins?" Holmes asked.

"Her father, by the name of Enoch Bell made his money grubbing for gold on the West Coast of the United States. He 'struck it rich', if I may use a vulgar Americanism, in California, and plucked his daughter from the low saloon in which she was demonstrating unlikely poses as Betsy Belle, *tableaux vivants* artiste, and set her up as a hotel owner in New York. The hotel was a high-toned if shady casino and bordello."

Pike smiled. "Sir Edmund went to New York while on an antiquities hunt, met Betsy and was conquered."

"What does your nose say, Pike?" Holmes asked.

Pike sipped his tea and considered. "There is perhaps a slight swirl of something. There is the faintest rumour

Madame deGascoigne's manager may be a good manager, but he is in an interesting relationship with the lady."

"Deplorable," I exclaimed.

"The son?"

"A vacuous nincompoop of the sort that strong mothers and soft fathers often rear. He lolls at Oxford in his first year of reading wine labels. He is almost twenty, a year from his majority."

"How convenient was Sir Edmund's passing?" Holmes asked.

Pike pursed his lips. "The old buffer was planning another trip to the Valley of the Kings; that would have been expensive, but not a serious dent in the family fortune.

"However, he was also bidding high and higher at antiquities auctions here and in America. That drain on family finances could be a motive."

Pike shrugged. "He was sixty-two after all, a drunkard and, as he thought himself, a second Don Juan. He died at his club at the luncheon hour. The cottage pie, which several prominent members had specifically requested, was suspected and withdrawn, causing disquiet and ill-feeling."

Pike tapped a gloved finger against his lips. "I've heard nothing to implicate the wife. She has been scrabbling after honours for the poor fellow for the last several years."

"*Cui bono?*"

"Who benefits? A provision of the marriage contract was that the son by Sir Edmund's first marriage, the idiot Charlie, inherits if there was no later issue. Poor Sir Edmund did not quite manage another heir before he was called to the Other Side."

"Lady deGascoigne is protective of her stepson."

"Naturally," Pike answered. "Her husband's money and (by an oversight of her lawyers) her own dowry will soon be in his dim-witted hands. But an astonishing amount went to the butler. I hear it was an unbelievable ten thousand pounds. What can he have done to merit such a sum?"

"Let's get a four-wheeler to the Museum, Watson. My nose suggests rain is on the way." We caught a passing growler and, as Holmes had predicted, rain was pattering on the roof by the time we passed Piccadilly.

"I'm a little confused, Holmes. What does Lady deGascoigne expect from us for her money?"

"The missing mummy."

"But why is she so bothered?" I asked. "It is a British Museum problem if they accepted and signed for the delivery. Why did she engage you in the matter?"

"I have no idea."

A policeman directed our cab to one of the back entrances to the Museum where a uniformed attendant instructed our cabby to park in the yard under a lean-to roof. The attendant asked us our business, then guided us through a side door, along labyrinthine, dimly lit passages and up several sets of stairs.

"You'll be Scotland Yard detectives, then," he said in a broad West Country accent, turning back to Holmes as he led us along a corridor with suites of offices and workshops on either side.

"Not exactly—" I answered, but Holmes overrode me.

"A baddish business, this, by all accounts," he said, tapping his nose with his finger in a gesture that brought Inspector Lestrade to my mind.

The attendant stopped at an office door. "Jabez Rawlins is a good man, gentlemen, not given to apparitions and delusions. He is Band of Hope, pledged in my sight at our mission in Falmouth. He's not touched a drop of alcohol since his wife and son passed over these ten years past."

"We will take that into consideration," Holmes said in a serious tone.

"Just so you know." The attendant knocked and opened the door.

A thin, balding man looked up from a sheaf of papers on his desk and regarded Holmes over his gold *pince-nez*.

"Detectives," the attendant said, ushering us into the room and closing the door behind us.

The man at the desk blinked up at Holmes and made no move to stand or greet us.

Holmes took off his hat and hooked it onto a hat rack. "I am Sherlock Holmes, the consulting detective, and this is my companion Doctor Watson. We act for Lady deGascoigne. You must be Mr Darling."

Mr Darling gave Holmes a cold look. "A telegram came this morning from Lady deGascoigne requesting an interview at five pm. I replied saying the matter at issue had been resolved and there was no need for any further discussion or correspondence. No need for this meeting in fact."

The clock on the mantel chimed five and Mr Darling stood, took his hat and umbrella from the hat stand and picked up his keys. "I am sorry you gentlemen have been inconvenienced. I will show you out—"

Holmes sat on a chair in front of the desk and shook a cigar from his packet. "There is just the matter of Rawlins and the apparition."

Mr Darling sighed. He replaced his hat and umbrella, pocketed his keys and sat once more behind his desk. I took the chair beside Holmes as he lit his cigar with a match.

Mr Darling sighed again. "I do not know how—"

Holmes held up his hand. "It is my business to know. Let us go through the matter from the beginning. Doctor Watson and I are here to help."

Mr Darling looked down at his desk. "I am not – the outcry if it got out! No, no, I am sorry Mr Holmes—" He stood and glanced again at the clock on the mantel.

"We will not take up much of your time," Holmes said. "And we have a growler waiting at the Museum gate that will get you to the Haymarket in time for your appointment."

Mr Darling paled and subsided into his chair. He looked from Holmes to me, wide-eyed in astonishment.

"It's our business to know," I reminded him.

Mr Darling shook his head. "If you already – well, very well." He looked up and sighed again. "So, gentlemen, very well, well indeed, but I must ask for your solemn assurance anything I tell you will go no further, especially not to Lady deGascoigne. High words were exchanged during her last visit, words I would not repeat even in our exclusively male company."

He blinked at us through his spectacles.

"I cannot promise that, Mr Darling," Holmes replied. "We are the lady's agents in this case. But I will engage to request Lady deGascoigne refrain from seeking to address you on the matter."

"And that she does not come here," Mr Darling said vehemently. "Not ever again."

"Agreed."

"Good." Mr Darling nodded to himself. "I am a sensitive man, gentlemen, as I do not mind admitting. Mine is a gentle, cultured soul, happier perhaps in the eighteenth dynasty at Luxor than in modern London. I do not suppose reincarnation is an interest of – no, I cannot expect it, no, no, of course not."

He nodded to himself again. "Well then, as long as the provisions we have discussed are clear: no visits, that is the crux."

"The facts, Mr Darling, if you please," Holmes said softly. "If I am to be of any use to you, I must have data."

Mr Darling seemed to gather resolution. "We received several cartloads of antiquities donated to the Museum by Sir Edmund deGascoigne. He was not what you would call a scholarly man, but he had taste and ample funds. His butler, Bowen, on the other hand is well-read and has a most systematic mind for a person of his class and limited education. He advised his master well, and the collection is a notable one."

Mr Darling nodded to himself and muttered something under his breath I could not catch.

"On arrival, the larger items (the mummies and some items of furniture) were placed in storerooms on this floor of the Museum, and the jewellery and smaller carvings were locked in my safe." He indicated a large green and gold Chubb safe that stood against the wall.

"On Monday, as we began a catalogue of the items, I heard from one of my clerks that the night attendant in the storerooms along the corridor had been found by his daytime colleagues as they arrived for work that morning in a dazed and incoherent state. He claimed he had seen a spirit or ghost, and it had attacked him."

Mr Darling pursed his lips in distaste. "I assumed he was in drink."

"Mr Rawlins is Band of Hope and fiercely temperance," said Holmes.

Mr Darling frowned. "I did not know. I instructed the supervisor to admonish him and send him home on four days' suspension. I shall make a note to investigate further."

He dipped his nib in the inkpot, wrote a line or two in a small notebook or diary, blotted it and looked up again. "The following day, we completed our inventory of the deGascoigne jewellery and started on the larger items of the collection. Each mummy case was opened under my personal supervision to ensure the type and condition of the contents were correctly indicated in the manifest. The third case we examined was empty apart from wood shavings and other rubbish."

He leaned back in his seat and glanced at the clock. "I wrote a note to lady deGascoigne apprising her of that fact. Would you gentlemen care for a whisky?"

Mr Darling took a bottle and three glasses from a drawer and poured Scotch into tumblers. "I keep whisky here for medicinal purposes."

Holmes took two glasses of whisky, passed one to me and nodded for Mr Darling to go on.

"My note prompted Her Ladyship to visit this office," Mr Darling continued in a soft voice. "She expressed her dissatisfaction with the Department's custodianship of her husband's collection and demanded we hand it back. Certain words were spoken to me in a low American idiom with which I am wholly unfamiliar."

He dabbed at his brow with his handkerchief. "I received a telegram this morning demanding a further interview with her or her agents with understandable apprehension. I feared another scene would inevitably ensue. I could not submit myself to such an ordeal. You should understand no women are employed in my department, none at all. I am unused to vehemence from the fair sex (I am unmarried). It unnerved me."

Mr Darling mopped his brow again. "I immediately replied that the matter was under official investigation and no further communication need be exchanged until the discrepancy was resolved.

"Was it?"

"Under investigation? No. But I do not consider the missing item to be particularly important; things do get mislaid, even large things. The mummy was that of a minor priest of the Temu cult at Heliopolis during the reign of Pami, a twenty-second dynasty pharaoh who ruled for a short time, around 770 BC. It presented no important distinguishing characteristics compared to a score of similar mummies from the period."

Mr Darling leaned across his desk. "If I might make an uncharacteristically controversial statement, gentlemen, my firm opinion is that progress in this century in many scientific disciplines and even more in social organisation has reached a point of perfection rendering further research in most cases superfluous. Mummies are a drug on the market. The Pami mummy is in that class. It has no distinctive features."

"Except that it is missing," said Holmes.

Mr Darling took a sip of whisky. "I do not like to use that word, Mr Holmes. In the hands of the sensational press—"

"The headline, 'Missing Mummy Loose in London', springs to mind," Holmes said. "People would be alarmed."

"It would provoke a mass panic," I said. "Worse than a rumour that Spring Heeled Jack was prowling the streets."

"Indeed," Mr Darling said, wiping his hands with his handkerchief. "That is exactly the reaction I fear the gutter press would ignite.

"The director of the Museum abhors public scrutiny, as do I. Our clear duty is to put a stop to any further speculation on the matter."

Mr Darling shook his head. "The mob's fear of mummy attack is illogical. Mummies have not only been dead for many centuries, they are missing vital organs, including brains! And they are so trussed in bandages that movement of any sort, let alone violent attack, would be impossible. However, the mob's terror does not derive from a logical source. The lower orders are swayed by the penny dreadful papers and rabble-rousing preachers, many of whom are of foreign extraction."

Holmes and I digested Mr Darling's views in a long silence.

"How would you value the collection?" Holmes asked at last.

Mr Darling leaned back in his chair as he considered. "The mummies have a certain value to collectors (and to carnival and freak show exhibitors) and then there is the jewellery. That has a considerable value. I was not surprised Lloyds insured the collection in the sum of ten thousand pounds, of which the precious items account for eight thousand. The insurance companies have closer links to collectors than we have, and they have their fingers on the pulse of the market; the true value may be higher."

"Do you keep the jewellery here?" Holmes gestured to the safe in the corner of the office.

"For now, while we are cataloguing, yes. The items will then be stored in our strongrooms in the basement."

"And you will prepare them for exhibition?"

Mr Darling sniffed. "In the fullness of time. As you may imagine Mr Holmes, we have in the Museum a huge collection of artefacts from every age and continent. The pieces we can put on show to the public form a small or even a tiny proportion of the whole. It is possible we might mount a special Egyptian exhibition at some later date, and a few items may be on display, but I do not think it at all likely, not for several years, or tens of years, at the very least. The collection will be available to scholars, of course."

He smiled a condescending smile. "You realise the British Museum has been open, gratis, for just six years. I cannot believe the public has assimilated much from the current collections in that short time. One cannot expect persons of limited understanding and education to appreciate even the few items we have room to exhibit – I am sure you get my drift, gentlemen."

"Of course," said Holmes. "Would it be possible to view the jewels?"

Mr Darling glanced at the clock, sighed and reached into his pocket for his keys. Holmes and I watched as he knelt at the safe, inserted two long brass keys one after the other into two key holes and turned them. He swung the door open and extracted a large cardboard box. He took off the lid, removed a half-dozen trays lined with black velvet and laid them across his desk.

The effect was overwhelming. Each tray exhibited a scintillation of glittering highlights from coloured gems in fabulous settings of gold and enamel. There were scarab rings, Eye-of-Horus brooches, gold neckpieces and fabulous multi-stranded necklaces of precious stones and beads. Many pieces were adorned with large jewels set in gold in the shape of cats, snakes and the ubiquitous ankh cross. It was a most impressive collection.

"We are beholding eight thousand pounds worth of jewels," I said, entranced.

"So say Lloyds." Mr Darling returned the items to the box, the box to the safe and locked the door.

"They are perfectly secure, here. My safe is one of the most modern Chubbs, installed just two years ago and guaranteed thief-proof."

He held up the two keys. "I keep these on my watch chain, which never leaves my person, or at least my sight. The only other keys are with Sir Edward Bond, the Principal Librarian."

To Mr Darling's astonishment, Holmes seized the keys, whipped out his magnifying glass and examined them.

"They are manufactured by Chubb by a patented process that makes them impossible to duplicate," Mr Darling said with a smug sniff. "And the locks are guaranteed burglar-pick-proof by the company."

"They look complicated," Holmes said, returning the keys.

Mr Darling clipped them back on his watch chain and looked again at the clock.

Holmes stood. "We shall take up no more of your time, sir. You have been most informative."

"Not at all." Mr Darling darted out from behind his desk to shake our hands and grab his coat, hat and stick.

"You may need your umbrella," I suggested. "It is raining cats and dogs."

"One more thing, Mr Darling," Holmes said as we were ushered out into the corridor. "Would you have an address for the night attendant, Mr Rawlins?"

"I can do better than that, sir, I can direct you to him. His suspension ended yesterday, and he is working tonight. I checked with his supervisor that he arrived on time and sober."

Mr Darling led us to a large room filled with sets of shelves piled with boxes and paper-wrapped parcels.

"There is no need for you to wait, Mr Darling," Holmes said solicitously. "You can take our cab; they will be hard to come by in the rain. Let me see, one and thruppence, plus thirty minutes waiting, call it three and six, including tip. Give the Assistant Curator four bob, Watson, fair's fair."

Holmes looked on benignly as I passed Mr Darling the coins. "By the way," he said, "in your conversation with Lady deGascoigne the other day, did my name come up at all?"

Mr Darling blinked at him and blushed bright red.

"It is of no consequence, sir. Have a pleasant evening."

"Rawlins will have to see you out, as the museum regulations allow no unescorted visitors after closing time," Mr Darling said. "He is the attendant seated over there by the window."

We said our goodbyes and approached a heavily built, rather plump man in attendant's uniform sitting on a chair set against a curtain-lined wall. Beside him was a row of decorated mummy cases. At his feet was a long, grey chisel.

He stood and drew himself to attention as we approached.

"Good evening, Rawlins." Holmes introduced us, explaining we were acting with the permission of Assistant Curator Darling. Holmes smiled. "In fact, we have already spoken with Mr Darling and informed him you are a member of the Band of Hope temperance society and no drunk."

"I'm not just temperance, sir, I'm teetotal," Rawlins said. "I am a total abstinent. I shun all liquors and made beverages including beer, tea and coffee. There is no such thing as moderation in imbibing the Devil's Brew, gentlemen, that is my settled opinion."

Holmes nodded. "I'm sure there is a good deal of sense in what you say. Tell us about that night, the night you were attacked."

"It was last Sunday. I was sat just over there, sir, having my bit of cold beef and bread washed down with God's own beverage."

He looked expectantly at me.

"Water," I suggested.

"Water, sirs. That, not bread, is the staff of life. Suddenly, I saw a shadow move across that bronze plate, the one hanging on the wall by the windows. You can see it plain in the lamplight."

"Show us where you sat on that night," Holmes requested.

Rawlins slipped the chisel into his trouser pocket, picked up his chair and placed it by one of the long racks filled with Egyptian items.

"I was sat right here, sirs. See how the light from the lamp gleams in the bronze, eh? I saw a shadow, and I heard a faint creak from over there."

He pointed towards the line of mummy cases leaning against the curtained wall.

"I turned my head, and one of the mummy cases moved, sirs. Something inside it was pushing the lid up, trying to get out."

Rawlins looked at us, wide-eyed. "You may imagine, gents, that I was frozen solid with my sandwich halfway to my mouth. I saw the case open and a small, dark figure slip out. It looked around (I noticed the glimmer of its eyes) and it stretched, like it had been cramped in the case for a long time."

"Twenty-second Dynasty," Holmes mused. "Two thousand five hundred years, give or take a few centuries. No wonder it was a little stiff in the joints. Continue, Mr Rawlins."

"It crept along the wall, opened the curtains and looked through the windows, staring at the moon."

Holmes frowned. "That is interesting."

"I stood, and my foot hit against something and made a noise. When I looked around, the figure had gone."

"What time did this occur?" Holmes asked.

"At about eight or eight-fifteen sir, when I have my dinner break of a night."

"An early rising mummy then, Watson. Midnight is the usual hour for the manifestation of ghouls." Holmes turned back to Rawlins. "How many other watchmen patrol the Museum? Are you armed?"

"At least one for every floor of the wings, sir. And maybe more guarding the vaults. We are all equipped with lanterns, police rattles and whistles."

He patted the chisel sticking out of his pocket. "And I have something will give the little beggar pause if he tries his capers again. Jabez Rawlins will not be caught out twice."

"Show me how the mummy looked up at the moon, will you?"

Rawlins led us to the wall and pulled back a thick curtain to reveal high windows with separate skylights. He gazed up through one of the windows, moving his head from side to side.

"That's how it looked, wagging its head. I saw it clear in silhouette, sir, with the moonlight and the glow from the street lamps. I could see bits of bandage hanging from its arms."

"Do these long windows, or the upper skylights open?" Holmes asked.

"I'm not sure, sir. I've never seen them open, so I'd say not. It would not be good for the antiquities to let in the sunshine or the noxious air of London."

Holmes held his pocket watch to the oil lamp that hung on a bracket from the wall. "It is now five-forty and clouds hide the moon, but calculating five days declination and two hours or so later, the moon would have been – light please, Rawlins."

Holmes jotted figures on his shirt cuff. He nodded to himself and pointed up towards the skylight. "There, call it fifty-six degrees, just waning, the full moon was a week ago."

He shone Rawlins' lamp up at the skylight. "An energetic man or mummy could find a way up to and along the curtain rail."

He examined the ranges of shelves by the wall and leapt up onto one.

"I say, Holmes, do take care." I admonished my friend without hope he would take notice.

The attendant watched wide-eyed as Holmes clambered up the shelves, leapt across the gap between them and the windows and hung from the lamp bracket. He levered himself up, stood on the bracket and examined the skylight for a moment before he pulled on a catch. The window dropped open a few inches.

"Not wide enough for a man, but enough for a smallish mummy," he said. "They shrink in the drying process."

Holmes peered at the glass and metal framing. "This skylight is smudged with hand and foot prints, while the neighbouring frames are clear. Hello?"

He picked something from the frame and pocketed it. I felt a surge of relief as he dropped back down.

Rawlins blinked in astonishment as Holmes grabbed the attendant's lantern again and knelt, glaring at the floor through his magnifying glass.

"We are in luck, Watson." He slipped some fibres into a small envelope, stood and turned to the attendant. "Rawlins, you say you were attacked by the figure?"

"I can only assume so, sir. I remember nothing. I was found by the door, bleeding, dazed and barely conscious."

"My colleague is a doctor; may he examine you?"

Rawlins drew himself up. "I am a Christian Scientist, sir. I believe in the power of prayer as the only healing agent."

"Doctor Watson will guarantee to look at your skull and make no medical observations within your hearing. He will prescribe no medicine whatsoever for you." He turned to me. "Do you undertake to abide by those rules, Doctor?"

"I suppose I do."

Rawlins reluctantly took off his attendant's cap, and I examined his head. I nodded to Holmes.

"Now," he said, moving to the row of mummy cases and pointing to one. "Was this the case from which the mummy escaped?"

"Indeed, sir. How did you know?" Rawlins answered.

Holmes opened the lid. "It is my business to know. Light."

The case contained not a mummy, but a woven reed basket and a length of thin rope. Holmes took each item out and examined it. "Modern basket and rope, Watson, ha!"

"How do you know, Holmes?" I said, echoing the attendant.

"It is my business – oh very well. The rope is brand-new Manila of the type recently developed for peak-climbing."

He held the basket upside down under my nose in the lamplight.

"I see strange characters," I said. "Are they Egyptian hieroglyphs?"

"They are Japanese characters. The first is a one and the second, separated by a dash, a six. The flimsy rush basket cost a ridiculous one shilling and sixpence. At that price it must have come from the overpriced bazaar next to the Japanese Village in Knightsbridge."

He knelt and went through a pile of bits of cloth and fibres at the bottom of the mummy case. He held up a shred of bandage, reached into his pocket and pulled up another.

"Identical. Whatever was in that case was also up at the skylight." Holmes picked a pinch of brown fibres from the case and dropped them into a small envelope. "I would bet a guinea to a ha'penny that these rope shreds will match those on the floor."

"What is that, Holmes?" I said, pointing to something gleaming amid the rubbish. Holmes picked up a small jewel. "A gold tiepin with a small pearl."

"From the mummy?" I asked.

"I don't believe so, Watson. The Ancient Egyptians, lacking neckties and cravats, had little use for tiepins, and the hallmark is a horse head, is the mark of Paris, not Cairo. Write a receipt for the attendant, would you, and we shall be on our way?"

"It's after hours," Rawlins said. "I'll have to come down with you, sirs, at least as far as the man in the main lobby. He can get you a cab. It looks like the rain's eased."

He ushered us downstairs to the back door of the Museum where I gave him half a crown and shook his hand. He thanked me and then leaned towards me.

"I'll tell you a something, sir," he whispered, "something I dursen't tell the supervisor for fear he'd have me out the door and straight into Bedlam madhouse. When the morning shift found me on the floor, I had a bandage around my head, under my cap. Who saw to my wounds, I do not know. My fellow attendants swear they did not patch me up, so who did?"

"There is a large lump on Rawlins' head, and plenty of dried blood, Holmes," I said as we rattled towards Baker Street in a hansom. "He has not washed his hair this week. There is also blood on the inside of his cap. Mr Rawlins received a heavy blow to the head within the last few days. That much is certain."

"A vicious mummy, then."

"Rawlins says his head was then bandaged by person or persons unknown before his day-shift colleagues arrived."

"The mummy has a gentler side, it feels remorse. It is certainly an energetic fellow. It climbed up to the skylight; I saw its paw prints on the glass."

"You think it escaped through the window? That it is loose in the city?"

Holmes shrugged a Continental shrug.

"How did you know from which mummy case it escaped?" I asked.

"Mr Darling told us."

I considered. "Of course, he mentioned it was the third case they examined. They obviously started on the side nearest the entrance door."

"It seemed likely."

"An elementary deduction then."

Holmes did not deign to answer me.

We got home to find Wiggins, the teenaged leader of Holmes band of street Arab informers, asleep on the sofa.

Holmes woke him and poured him a whisky.

"I set the Irregulars on Lulu's brothel," Holmes said as he splashed in soda from the gasogene. "If the jewels are the mummy's target (and this mummy has exhibited a violent temperament and tender remorse, so why not avarice?) then it must wax the safe keys. Where better than at Lulu's, when Mr Darling is disrobed and his attention is elsewhere? I saw no traces of wax on Mr Darling's keys, therefore the mummy or its confederates had not yet gained access to them."

He handed the glass to Wiggins. "Report, young man."

"The mark was a boy, sir, about my age or a bit younger," said Wiggins. "He waited outside Lulu's till a cab came up with a top-hole gent who Madame greeted as Mr D.

"One of the ladies slipped the boy inside ten or fifteen minutes after the gent. He wasn't in Lulu's more than ten minutes before he came out and jumped into a cab. He got down at the corner of Great Dover street and Swan Street in the Borough, waited for the cab to take off before he strolled to the Dutchman's house as cool as you please."

Wiggins took a long slug of whisky. "Fifteen minutes later, he walked two streets to a cab rank and took another hansom. He got off at Drayson Mews and ducked around the corner to a villa on Kensington Church Street."

"He did not go to Knightsbridge?" Holmes asked.

"No, sir. He went in the front door of a prime villa opposite the park. A footman let him in and addressed him as Master Hugh."

Wiggins drained his glass, and Holmes gestured for me to get him another. I mixed a little whisky with a great deal of soda water and handed it to the boy.

"I went back to the Borough," Wiggins continued. "And I braced the Dutchman. He was clammed up tight until I mentioned your name, Mr Holmes, and then he became cooperative."

"I got him off a charge of handling stolen goods in eighty-three," Holmes said. "He was guilty, but the evidence against him was trifling, and I needed him for a certain matter connected with the affair of the aluminium crutch."

"I don't recall that case, Holmes," I said. "A crutch made of aluminium! That would have been extremely expensive."

"The crutch was fashioned by the Hollander at his premises in the Borough. He is a master metalsmith. He specialises in patent thief-proof padlocks and the implements to open them. Go on, Wiggins."

"Herr Hollander charged ten quid for two safe keys with a fiver deposit, and ten bob for a door key. The buyer required they be ready by noon, day after tomorrow."

Holmes smiled. "We are at the heart of a conspiracy, Watson, but we have no clear idea of the players involved. Who is this boy and what part does he have in the affair?"

"He is not Charlie deGascoigne?"

"We shall see."

We visited the deGascoigne townhouse in Knightsbridge the following morning. It was a fine Georgian structure set back from the road and reached by a curving gravel carriageway. Our cab set us outside the front door just as it opened and a tall, balding man in evening dress appeared in the doorway.

"Her ladyship is not at home, gentlemen," he said.

"Never mind, Bowen, we wish to talk to you," said Holmes.

The butler bowed and opened the door wide.

I instructed the cabby to wait and followed Holmes into an imposing hall with a sweeping staircase directly in front of the door and archways on either side. Bowen ushered us into a large circular room with a domed ceiling and empty niches in the walls.

"This is the ballroom, gentlemen. The collection was kept here. The mummies were housed in the alcoves and niches and the other items in rows of glass cases. The jewellery was displayed in cabinets in the next room."

Holmes nodded. "You know who we are and what we are here about."

"The missing mummy. You are Sherlock Holmes and the other gentleman is Doctor Watson. My mistress mentioned you might visit."

"Were there any anomalies in the shipment of the collection to the Museum?" Holmes asked.

"No, sir, all went well. I am at a loss to account for the missing item. I and the supervisor from the Egyptology Department kept meticulous records."

"Your son attends Harrow School," Holmes said, changing the subject.

Bowen seemed unfazed. "He did so until recently. He left a few days ago; a matter of money, gentleman. While he lived, Sir Edmund generously paid my boy's school expenses. His lordship's fee-payment and allowance were stopped on the day of his death.

"I am informed by Sir Edmund's solicitors I received a competence in his will that would enable me to continue my son's education, but I also understand the execution of the will is delayed by legal complications and the money may not be forthcoming for some time."

"Do you live here with your wife?" Holmes asked.

"My wife died in childbirth." Bowen indicated a thin black band around the cuff of his tail coat. "Fourteen years ago last March."

Holmes nodded. "I understand you are leaving Lady deGascoigne's employment. Will you apply for a position with another household?"

"That is possible, sir, but there are certain difficulties. Lady deGascoigne does not feel disposed to write me a character, and as you know gentlemen, without a character I shall not be considered for employment by a reputable house. I intend, when Sir Edmund's funds are released, to set up a small business specialising in travel to Egypt for antiquarian purposes. I speak the language (the modern Egyptian), and I have some knowledge of Ancient Egypt."

"Mr Darling at the British Museum spoke highly of your scholarship."

Bowen smiled. "That was kind of the gentleman. I was lucky enough to have access to Sir Edmund's fine library on the subject."

"Also donated to the Museum?" Holmes asked.

"No, the books are crated and awaiting shipment to the school in Little Rock, Arkansas in the United States Lady deGascoigne attended."

"Is there a faculty of Egyptian Studies there?" I asked.

Bowen smiled again. "I doubt it, Doctor. The school is a Methodist institution catering for pauper children from six to eleven."

I raised my eyebrows to Holmes. Lady deGascoigne clearly had a vindictive side to her character, or at the least a dark sense of humour.

"Do you know this?" Holmes held up the pearl tiepin.

Bowen frowned. "I think I do. It is like one belonging to Master Charlie, Sir Edmund's son. One of a pair; the other has a jet stone."

"The young man is at Oxford?" Holmes asked.

"Yes and no, sir. He is a student there, but he is upstairs, asleep. He had a late night out with his friends."

"When did he come down from college?"

"He's been here since the funeral, sir, for more than a week."

Holmes nodded. "Is there a photograph of the boy I could see?"

"Master Charlie? Yes, there are several in the morning room." Bowen led the way into a bright room with chintz-covered furniture that looked onto the back garden. He picked up a cabinet photograph of young men lolling on a lawn. "He's third from the left, the heavyset, blond boy."

A maid put her head around the door. "Master Charlie's bell, Mr Bowen. Ringing like there's no tomorrow."

"Thank you, Dottie." Bowen turned to me. "The young master will be wanting his breakfast."

I raised my eyebrows. "At eleven in the morning?"

Bowen bowed. "Will that be all, sirs? I must get on with my duties."

He led us back to the hall and picked up a tray that lay on a side table. On it were a glass and a wine cooler with a bottle of Champagne on ice. "Master Charlie will be impatient."

"By the way, Bowen, I imagine you have a day or half-day off every week?" Holmes asked.

"Sunday, sir, all day tomorrow. Sir Edmund made it a policy to give the staff leave to attend divine service and meditate in private on the Lord's Day."

"Thank you, Bowen. I may call on you again."

He bowed again. "A pleasure, gentlemen."

"I would suggest not much love is lost between Lady deGascoigne and her butler," I said as we clattered back down the path to the gatehouse in the cab. "Her Ladyship seems to have gone out of her way to humiliate Bowen."

"I wonder how Bowen behaved to his ill-educated mistress while he was a favourite of Sir Edmund's," Holmes said.

"A good point. Whatever the circumstances, Bowen may have to wait several years for his inheritance. Lady deGascoigne is in a position to delay or block it."

Billy met us at the door of our lodgings. "Inspector Lestrade called, sirs. I showed him upstairs to the sitting room."

Holmes led the way upstairs. "It might be a kindness if we make a little noise," he suggested. "We don't want to catch the inspector snooping."

We found Lestrade looking out of the window wearing an innocent expression.

"Ah, there you are, gentlemen," he said with a sly grin. "I have something to show you that might engage your interest." He indicated a large leather portmanteau on our dining table. He undid the three straps that held the portmanteau closed and flung open the lid with a conjurer's flourish. "What do you say to that, Mr Holmes?"

Inside the bag lay a shrivelled, blackened body. The skull was covered in matted black hair, yellow teeth protruded from flaky black lips and the eye sockets were empty. It was wrapped in grimy bandages and it exuded a most offensive smell.

"What an ugly brute," I exclaimed.

"It came out of the Thames Drag yesterday evening, Doctor. A gang of mudlarks found it washed ashore by The Grapes pub in Limehouse. They paraded the corpse up and down Narrow Street where it was seen by the landlord of the pub who bought it for half a crown and set it up on the bar counter as a curiosity. The local constable had a quiet word, and it was delivered to the mortuary for examination."

Lestrade turned to Holmes with something close to a comic leer. "Do you have any notion what it is, Mr Holmes? The coroner had seen nothing like it in thirty years' service."

Holmes picked his magnifying glass from his desk and subjected the corpse to an intensive examination. "It is an Egyptian mummy dating from the twenty-second Dynasty, let us say about seven centuries before Christ, in the reign of Pharaoh Pami. The body is of a minor priest of the cult of Temu at a temple in Heliopolis."

Lestrade sighed, shook his head and turned to me. "It's like the black magic, isn't it Doctor? Mr Holmes would have been burned at the stake a century or two ago."

"No jet tiepin is with the remains, Doctor," said Holmes. "Perhaps the mudlarks took it." He smiled at Lestrade. "I must, despite my promise to the Assistant Curator of the Egyptian department of the British Museum, acquaint you with strange happenings in their store rooms."

Holmes gave the inspector a short account of the escape of the mummy from its case.

Lestrade poked the mummy with his gloved finger. "This fellow does not appear capable of the agile feats you describe, Mr Holmes."

"You do not think the mummy entered the Thames of its own accord then, Inspector."

"I do not. Thrown off a bridge, most like."

Holmes pursed his lips. "By whom?"

"The Museum contains the treasures of the world, Mr Holmes. And collectors are by their nature acquisitive. I think I might take a sniff around the fences specialising in stolen art." The inspector closed his portmanteau and took his leave.

"What is the connection between the mummy and the moon, Holmes?" I asked as we settled back in our chairs. "Why was it looking at the moon? Was it a religious observance? Something associated with the god, Temu?"

"The mummy was looking not at the moon, but at the catch of the skylight window. It was wondering if the window could be opened. It could, and that is how it will make its escape."

I looked at Holmes in astonishment. "Escape, Holmes? It's in the portmanteau in Inspector Lestrade's carriage."

"No, Watson. The mummy never left the British Museum."

The following evening, Holmes and I huddled in a dark and chilly office on the ground floor of the Museum with windows facing both the front gate and the east side of the building.

"It's eight o'clock," I said as my watch chimed the hour.

"They are out there," said Holmes. "The policeman at the gate may be staying them. They are waiting for him to move on. Wait, who is that?"

A cab stopped beside the policeman guarding the Museum gates, and a young man or boy leaned out and asked him a question. The constable turned and pointed up Great Russell Street.

I glimpsed a figure in black race through the gates behind the constable, past our window and along the side of the Museum.

"It's coming off," said Holmes. "Quick now, upstairs as fast as we can, but don't alarm the guards."

We strode across the main hall and called a cheery greeting to the watchman to whom we had earlier shown our special pass, signed by Mr Darling, allowing us to wander the halls alone.

We hurried through a discrete door into the working areas of the building, then raced along dark corridors and up several flights of stairs to the corridor of the Egyptian Department. We halted and caught our breath outside Mr Darling's office. Light glimmered under the door. Holmes flung it open.

A boy dressed in mummy bandages looked up from where he sat in Mr Darling's chair. The cardboard jewel box and velvet-lined trays we had seen on our previous visit lay empty on the desk before him, and he was stuffing the last of the deGascoigne Egyptian jewels into his bag. Rawlins' chisel lay beside the empty box.

My eyes flicked to the corner of the room, and I saw the Chubb safe was open and two keys protruded from the keyholes.

"The door, Watson!" Holmes cried.

I lunged forward, and the boy darted past me, knocked me into the hat stand and slipped out the door, which slammed shut. I heard a key turn in the lock and a faint chuckle.

"I meant the office, not the safe door, old chap," Holmes said mildly. "Pass me the chisel. This is no time for half-measures." He jammed the heavy chisel into the gap between the office door and the jamb and heaved. There was a loud crack, and the door hung open.

We raced out along the corridor and into the store room. Rawlins sat on a chair in the middle of the room fast asleep and snoring.

The boy had pulled himself up a rope attached to the skylight, and he was in the act of climbing out. He looked back at us, grinned and waved his bag.

"Eddie, come down from there at once," Holmes ordered.

The boy frowned in astonishment and glared down at him. Holmes folded his arms and continued in a softer tone. "If you drop down to where your father is waiting, I shall spring the watchman's rattle. A constable is at the gate and more are on call. You, your father and possibly others will end up in prison."

The boy seemed to hesitate.

"We are not the police, young man. I am Sherlock Holmes, and this is my friend Doctor Watson. We mean you no harm. Come down and talk to us."

The boy blinked as he considered, then he climbed down and stood before us looking apprehensive. He was a slight, handsome boy with short brown hair and a milky complexion, looking absurd in his mummy wrappings. He laid the bag on the floor in front of him and Holmes pounced on it.

The boy held out his hand to me. "How do you do, Doctor?" he said in a cultured voice. "I am Eddie Bowen."

"You scared the living daylights out of me," I said, still panting from my exertions. "And you knocked me to the ground. I should put you over my knee and give you a good thrashing."

Eddie looked up at me with patently false expression of remorse. "I'm sorry, Doctor. I thought you were museum attendants. I only meant to escape from you. I may have pushed a little too hard. I box for my house, do you see?"

"Rawlins is out for the count; did you hit him?"

"No sir! That would not have been sporting. I drugged his water bottle when he went to the lavatory. I took his jemmy in case he woke up prematurely and was annoyed."

"Sporting? Pshaw!" I exclaimed. "Last week you attacked Rawlins from behind with a blunt instrument and you almost broke his head."

"Oh no, sir. When I saw him standing there with his sandwich in his hand, I roared at him and waved my bandages to scare him. He made a run for the door, tripped and slammed into the wall. You can see the dent his head made in the plaster. He knocked himself out. I checked he was breathing and wrapped his head with my bandages. I'd dressed as a mummy in case I was spotted."

I frowned. "You intended to leave the building after the theft by that high window. Why not drop from Mr Darling's windows? Why climb up there?" I asked.

"The office side has a row of lamp posts below it, sir."

Holmes held up an exquisite gold and enamel Eye of Horus on a thick gold chain. It gleamed in the lamplight.

"You hid in the store rooms," he said to Eddie, "sleeping by day and prowling by night for nearly a week. You were looking for weaknesses in the Museum security arrangements. The basket was for hauling up provisions and letting down your booty."

Eddie nodded. "That was the original plan."

"Who is the other boy?" Holmes asked. "The boy who had the keys made and distracted the constable?"

Eddie looked down at his toes. "It's not the done thing to peach on another chap, sir. Boys who do that are not well-regarded at Harrow."

Holmes wagged his finger. "I can find out. I know his first name is Hugh, and he lives in Kensington Church Street. I have no doubt he is a school friend of yours."

Eddie frowned. "Well then, he's the Hon. Hugh Cresswell, youngest son of the Baron Cresswell, the judge. He sits next to me in class. He thought it jolly hard cheese I had to leave the school, and he volunteered his help.

"The caper was his idea. He's very interested in crime, and he reads the police newspapers and all the books he can get on the subject. His first plan was for us to smuggle him into the Museum in the mummy case, so he could fiddle the safe open with his burglar kit. But when I overheard Lady deGascoigne discussing Mr Darling's lady friend with the other detective—"

"Mr Barker?" Holmes asked.

"Yes, sir. I thought I could get the keys and copy them while he was busy. Sir Edmund was a frequent visitor to Madame Lulu's. My father often had to pick his Lordship up from there when he'd had a few drinks too many, so he knows the girls. I sent a note in father's name to make the financial arrangements with Florrie. Hugh crept into the room, filched the office and safe keys while Mr Darling was occupied, made the wax impressions on the spot and returned the keys."

"Your friend Hugh is an active young man," I said.

"He aims to be a master criminal when he grows up, Doctor. A General Gordon of crime."

"And you? Do you also aim to continue your nefarious life?" I asked.

"I do not, sir. I intend to graduate with honours and help my father with his Egyptian travel business."

"Which university do the deGascoignes attend?" Holmes asked.

"New College, Oxford." Eddie answered. He reddened and looked down at his toes again.

"Bowen thinks his inheritance may be bogged down in the courts," said Holmes. "You, he and the General Gordon of crime put together an enterprise to finance your education and Bowen's business plans."

"My father knows nothing of this, sir!" Eddie cried.

"Ha! That is your second lie, young man. I am pleased to see you blush. I don't believe your mastermind Hugh was personally acquainted with the Hollander in the Borough with the key-making skills you required."

"Florrie told me—"

"Nonsense. You blush again. I also don't believe you overheard Barker and Lady deGascoigne or made the arrangement with the doxy at Madame Lulu's. Those arrangements were made by your father."

Holmes rubbed his hands together. "I believe I have all the details. Sir Edmund's fortune was estimated at forty thousand pounds on his death. He left Bowen ten thousand, one quarter of the whole. A magnificent sum. Correct?"

Eddie nodded.

"And the jewels have been assessed at eight thousand pounds," Holmes continued. He weighed the bag in his hand. "Do you have a buyer?"

"A collector who will pay ten thousand pounds."

Holmes considered. "Your customer must undertake to keep the collection intact and not to sell any part of it. He is to donate the gems to the British Museum in his will or to return them here within twenty years, whichever is the sooner. He, or his executor, may do so anonymously. Do you think your client would accept that proposal?"

"He is an elderly gentleman, sir, a well-regarded Egyptologist and an avid collector. He will not sell the gems."

"I say, Holmes—" I remonstrated.

"Very well, then," Holmes said, handing Eddie the bag. "Make use of the rope to remove yourself from our sight."

The boy hooked the bag over his shoulder and crossed to the window. He grabbed the rope.

"A moment, Eddie. The pearl tie-pin?" Holmes called.

Eddie hung his head. "I took it from Master Charlie's bedroom. He is a disagreeable fellow. I thought it would muddy the waters. I knew Charlie would not be arrested for the theft as he is a huge oaf and he'd not fit in the mummy case, so the suspicion wouldn't stick."

"The tie-pin confirmed the involvement of your household," Holmes said in an admonishing tone. "The pin could not have wafted into the case except through your father's agency – or yours. You must learn not to over-egg your pudding when planning a criminal enterprise; you might pass that advice on to Master Hugh."

The boy nodded, grinned, hauled himself up the rope and disappeared through the skylight.

Holmes turned to me and raised his eyebrows. "Well, Watson?"

"You know my feelings in these matters, Holmes," I said stiffly. "I shall revive the attendant."

"Yes, he made a brave, if somnolent attempt to prevent the robbery, but was overwhelmed. Sadly, we were also too late to catch the thief."

Holmes offered me his cigar case. "Eddie did well. The boy is not a fool, at least I hope he is not. His step-brother has not turned out well."

I struck a match and stopped. "Holmes?"

"Eddie, or shall we call him Edmund, is the natural son of Sir Edmund deGascoigne. The mother died in childbirth."

"The butler's wife."

Holmes nodded. "Sir Edmund paid his son's school fees and provided him, through Bowen, with a fine inheritance. No butler, however learned and useful about the house, or even in the Valley for the Kings, is worth ten thousand pounds."

"Lady deGascoigne threatened to delay the inheritance with legal actions. Do you think she knows about the boy, Holmes?"

Holmes held up his hand. "Rawlins is coming around, and I hear footsteps. That will be Lestrade with his troops. I had Wiggins send him a telegram."

Billy handed me the mail as Holmes and I sat down to breakfast the following day.

"Here is a note from Lady deGascoigne, Holmes."

He waved permission, and I opened the envelope. "She congratulates us on our success in returning the mummy to the Museum and wonders whether we have been engaged to retrieve the jewels. She encloses two cheques, each for a hundred guineas."

"Good." Holmes attacked his boiled egg with gusto.

I frowned. "But we did not recover the mummy, and we compounded the felonious theft of a fortune in jewels. How can we take this money?"

"We uncovered the who, the how and the why of the theft. That the mummy was found through the agency of the official police is neither here nor there. Would you rather give the cheques to the mudlarks who pulled it out of the Thames?"

Holmes passed me the coffee pot. "I must tell you, my dear friend, that there is such a thing as being too nice in such matters; it smacks of Continental enthusiasms and holier-than-thou Methodist obsessions. We'll see you in the Band of Hope and Christian Science next."

I considered. "No, Holmes. I shall donate my fee to the Chelsea Military Hospital."

"And I shall donate a part of mine to the Café Royal this evening. I have booked a table for eight o'clock. As it is the festive season, I ordered a roast goose. You may join me or content yourself with a crust of dry bread and a smear of dripping here in your lonely garret. I invited Langdale Pike to join us. We have lots of grist for his gossip mill."

"The matter of the natural child, Eddie?"

Holmes nodded. "Not for public consumption, for his private ear as a thank-you for his help. Pike thrives on gossip. And I shall lay odds with him on the date of the wedding."

I frowned.

"The nuptials of Lady deGascoigne and her ex-butler, Mr Bowen," said Holmes. "They were in it together, 'in cahoots' as the Americans have it. That nonsense with the delay in the inheritance, no character and the books sent to the lady's pauper school savoured too much of melodrama. Madame is far too pragmatic for that. And my arch-rival Barker would never allow himself to be overheard in such a casual fashion."

He smiled. "Betsy Belle will discard a nincompoop son and gain one worthy of her hopes and expectations."

I laughed. "She guessed Eddie was her husband's natural son?"

"Oh, yes, Watson, the resemblance was obvious to the trained or highly interested observer. The boy has his father's ears, but he is better endowed between them. I expect a Lord deGascoigne-Bowen to take his place among the peers in the House of Lords within a decade or two. Betsy Belle is a tenacious woman."

I frowned. "But if she was involved in the plot, why did she engage us to find the mummy?"

"Mr Darling intimated to her he had already contacted us. It was an understandable defensive overstatement on his part; he was on the ropes with Lady deGascoigne about to administer the *coup de grâce*. He made up a story I was investigating the case of the missing mummy to fend his antagonist off. Pass the coffee, old man."

I poured Holmes the last half-cup of coffee.

"Lady deGascoigne therefore approached us with what amounts to a bribe," he continued. "She paid us to look the other way; which we did, but not on her behalf. I would far rather the jewels were with someone who appreciates them than in the safe of the desiccated Mr Darling. The nation will get them in due course; there is no particular hurry."

"And what of the General Gordon of crime?" I asked.

"Young Hugh will come to our attention again in a few years," Holmes said. "I sent the boy copies of my monographs on footprints, ears and tobacco ash with an admonition to study them closely. We must give him a sporting chance against me."

THE RECKONING OF KIT MARLOWE

"I say Holmes, this is confounded odd. We are invited to a séance."

Holmes flicked down a corner of his afternoon newspaper and gave me a cold look. "That is what comes of accepting these wildly improbable cases of vampires, sibyls and skulls. We shall soon have Mrs Weldon and her Indian spirit guide knocking at our door demanding we validate their levitating tables and spectral trumpets. There is a pretty little murder case in Brompton I am sure Inspector Lestrade will ask me to consult on: I want nothing of your séance."

He snapped his newspaper to the next page and continued reading.

I slipped the telegram onto the dining table and maintained an attitude of silent rebuke. Curiosity may have killed the cat, but I knew inquisitiveness was a fundamental characteristic of the detective mind, however high-bred the individual concerned.

"Well?" Holmes said from behind his paper.

"The telegram is from Doctor Arthur Conan Doyle."

The corner of the paper came down again and Holmes gave me a quizzical look.

"He's a friend of a friend. I have only told you of him a dozen or more times."

"The poor chap with the mad father," Holmes said.

"He does not talk of him, but yes. Doctor Doyle is an expert on Mormonism and that is how we met. I wanted information on the Mormons as background to my notes on your Utah Territory case, and I was told Doyle has an interest in strange cults. I completed a draft of the story, and he was kind enough to read it and comment on matters relating to Utah and the Mormon Church. He returned the text today, followed by a telegram inviting us to a séance to be held this evening at eight under the auspices of Admiral Marlowe of the Greenwich Naval Academy."

I stood and looked out of the window. The oily brown fog that had obscured the houses opposite that morning was by late afternoon a thorough pea-souper. I could see nothing of the street through the greasy, clammy windows, even though the gas lamps had been lit early.

"We are invited to supper afterwards, but it would be a devil of a job getting to the Admiral's house in this weather."

"Tonight, did you say, Watson?" Holmes said. "That is impossible. I have arranged with Mrs Hudson that I have sole use of our tin bathtub for the evening, filled to the brim with piping-hot water. I intend to wallow, defying the fog and smoking my new pipe, much like a second Marat."

"Marat, Holmes? Was he not stabbed to death in his bath by a lady Girondist?"

"Exactly. And it was by a single stab wound the Brompton victim met his end."

"Shall I suggest tomorrow as a more convenient time for the séance, then?" I suggested with a smile.

Holmes returned my smile. "The weather is so gloomy I thought we might forsake the city and go to Brighton for the weekend. You are looking peaky, Watson. Can I not persuade you to accompany me? The sea air—"

"—And the Brighton dismemberment case I read about in this morning's papers."

Holmes turned back to his newspaper as the doorbell rang. I looked down into the street, but in the thick fog I could see only the vague shape of a carriage at the kerb. I heard heavy steps on the staircase and our page, Billy, opened the door for a familiar figure.

"Hello, Inspector," I said.

"Good afternoon," Lestrade said, shaking my hand and slumping onto his usual place on the sofa. "Or at least I could wish it a good afternoon. It's a right London particular, gentlemen, and my nose says it's in for a day or two at the least."

"We thought of going to Brighton," I said mischievously.

"The dismemberment? Yes, well, you won't get me eating seafood or pork anywhere on the South Coast for a week or more, what with the recent storms in the Channel, the wrecks and the murder."

Holmes and I blinked at each other.

"It's a trifle early, but perhaps I could offer you a whisky, Inspector?" I suggested.

"Very kind, Doctor. I have need of something to steady my nerves. And I must confess, gentlemen, I hope I might persuade you to postpone your excursion and come with me to Brompton this evening. It is as strange a case as I have ever come across, and it has me stumped."

I passed whiskies and soda to Holmes and Lestrade, then settled myself in my chair.

"I have an outline of the case, Inspector," Holmes said, indicating the afternoon paper on the carpet beside him. "Earlier today, a young man was stabbed in his bedroom at the parental home, a villa near the Boltons in Brompton."

Holmes sniffed. "The reporter conveyed that fact and one other as the only items of data in two columns and a half of newsprint. The second datum is the young man's name was Christopher Marlowe, son of Admiral Marlowe of the Greenwich Naval Academy."

"Eh? But Admiral Marlowe is the person holding the séance, Holmes!" I exclaimed.

Holmes raised his eyebrows in mock surprise. "What a strange coincidence."

"The man's name is a very important fact, Mr Holmes," Lestrade said, consulting his notes.

Holmes held up his hand. "Just a moment, Inspector."

He turned to me. "The Index, if you please, Watson: Admiral Marlowe."

I took down the relevant volume of Holmes' collection of scrapbooks containing newspaper and magazine articles, references and notes on an enormous range of subjects.

"We have 'Marlowe, Christopher, Elizabethan poet and dramatist.' And that is all; there are no other Marlowe entries."

The paucity of information on the admiral reflected, I thought, Holmes' lack of interest in military and naval matters. I was surprised he had an entry for the poet, as his knowledge of literature was patchy to say the least.

Holmes lit his new churchwarden pipe with a match. "Inspector, we must fortify you again to ensure a clear recitation of the strange events to which you have alluded. I see something has disturbed the iron frame of your constitution to the extent you are quite pale."

I refilled the Inspector's glass.

"Very kind, Doctor." Lestrade took a gulp of whisky. "I don't mind admitting to you gentlemen I feel pale. What happened today will haunt me for the rest of my life, and that is no exaggeration. You will have read the basic facts in the papers, but, by heaven, I've never known such a bizarre set of circumstances for a death in my entire career. It would be laughed off the stage at the Alhambra."

Holmes leaned forward, rested his elbows on the arms of his chair and steepled his fingers as the inspector assembled his thoughts. "From the beginning," Holmes said gently.

"Well, sir, I visited B Division of the Metropolitan Police in Brompton at ten this morning," Lestrade began. "I had a police photographer with me as I'd been ordered to arrange for photographic copies to be taken of the records of Walsh, the poisoner of the Sanderson family, as there was doubt as to the identity of the persons who lodged in the family home. We know Walsh did the deed, but that tiny doubt got the bugger off (pardon my French). We'd completed our work, and we were having a cup of tea with the duty sergeant when a boy appeared before the counter, distraught and tearful. He gave his name as William Christopher Marlowe, the son of Admiral Sir James Marlowe, retired, and said his brother had been stabbed and killed by persons unknown. He had bicycled from his family's villa nearby to acquaint the police with news of the tragedy.

"They were shorthanded at B Division, so I volunteered myself and the photographer to accompany the boy and a pair of constables to the scene. We engaged a four-wheeler and followed the lad through wisps and billows of fog to a large house set back from the Cromwell Road.

"I was introduced to Admiral Marlowe in the Library. Lady Marlowe had taken to her bed in understandable distress. Then I was shown to the son's bedroom by the butler, Frazer. He too was in a state, shaking with grief. He unlocked the door, and I surveyed the room from the doorway, getting a feel, as we might say, Mr Holmes."

Holmes nodded. "We might, Inspector."

"The room was small, with dark, panelled wood on the walls and on the ceiling. A four-poster bed stood against the outside wall. There were two windows, one on either side of the bed, both tight shuttered and bolted. A single oil lamp on a bedside table the only light, and below it on the floor and beside the bed, lay the body of a boy or a young man, nineteen, as I understood from the butler, Frazer, who was openly weeping.

"A veritable lake of blood surrounded the body. I moved closer and saw the hilt of a dagger protruded from the right eye of the corpse. I established Frazer had discovered his young master that morning when he noticed the breakfast tray, left as usual on a table outside the bedroom door by the maid at nine, was still untouched a half-hour later. Note that only the butler, the housekeeper and young Christopher had a key to his room, and it was habitually kept locked."

"The windows were also locked you say?"

"Shuttered and bolted from the inside, Mr Holmes. And there was no means of entry into the room other than the door (locked when Frazer opened it) and the bolted windows."

"Nine o'clock," I said. "The young man was a late-riser."

"According to the newspaper report, he'd just come down from the Michaelmas Term at Cambridge," said Holmes. "Indolence is a defining characteristic of university students. Carry on, Inspector."

"I went through the motions, gentlemen, although it was clear the boy was dead. I did not touch the body as I wanted to be sure that its position and aspect were properly recorded by my photographer. He took five or six plates before I ventured to examine the scene more particularly. The blood was also a factor."

"Excellent," said Holmes. "Do you happen to—"

Inspector Lestrade laid a brown folder onto the table. Holmes pounced on it and slid out a sheaf of photographs.

"The Admiral's sons were both photography aficionados, and they have a darkroom in a corner of the house our man said is superior in every respect to that of the Yard. He developed the pictures on-the-site, as it were. That was a piece of luck we thought, as the fog had thickened to its present state, and neither of us fancied a trip to Whitehall and back in this muck."

The door opened, Mrs Hudson bustled in with the tea things, and Billy came in behind her with a bucket of coal.

"You are very much underfoot, Madam," Holmes said as he rescued the photographs from the table. "I did not order tea, and to my certain knowledge Watson did not do so. Yet you encumber us with your cups and seedcake."

"It is the customary hour, old man," I remonstrated. "Is there really seedcake?"

Billy put the bucket beside the fire and Mrs Hudson ushered him out and left us to manage tea ourselves. I served Lestrade and helped myself to a cup of tea and a slice of cake as Holmes pored over the photographs with his magnifying glass.

"What do you see?" Holmes passed me a picture, and I settled back in my seat and held it to a lamp.

"A body next to the bed, very much as the Inspector described."

"What is he wearing?"

"A dark suit, shirt and tie, nothing unusual."

He handed me a sheaf of photographs, and from them I described the bedroom in much the same terms Lestrade had used. It seemed dark and austere for a young man, but I thought, as he had recently come down from the University, he might not have unpacked his private things.

Holmes gave me a final photograph. It was extraordinary. It showed the body in the same position as in the previous shots, but visible, although faintly outlined, was another figure, who seemed to float above the corpse, smiling. The figure was dressed in clothes I would have associated with the reign of Elizabeth, or perhaps James 1. He had a mop of hair framing a broad pale face with arched eyebrows, a thin, downward turned moustache and a wisp of beard.

"I don't understand, Holmes. Who is this strange apparition?"

"Let me see if I can piece together the events of the morning, Inspector," Holmes said, rubbing his hands together. "Your man took photographs of the body and the room. He retired to the developing room—"

"Dark room," I corrected.

"—and he *developed* the pictures he had taken. I understand the process involves springing a light through the glass plate onto prepared paper, then dousing the paper with chemicals, washing the photographs and hanging them up to dry."

"There is more to it than that, old chap," I suggested. "First the plate has to be—"

"I would imagine," Holmes overrode me, "your photographer took a rest from his labours while the prints dried."

"He joined me and the younger son for coffee in the Library," Lestrade answered.

"Served by?"

"I'm not sure what you mean, Mr Holmes. Coffee was served by maids. I did not take their names."

"After your coffee, the photographer collected the prints, and you pored over them," Holmes said. "I can well imagine your shock when you saw a spectral figure standing over the corpse."

"It was a shock, sir. I'll not deny it. I showed the photograph to the younger son, Will, who identified—"

"Christopher Marlowe, Elizabethan poet and dramatist." Lestrade nodded sheepishly.

"You ordered your photographer to examine the plate and to make another photograph from it," Holmes said. "It is free of Elizabethan Marlowes."

Lestrade nodded again. "I sent him back to the Yard to print further copies using our official equipment. We'll not see anything of him until the morning, not if this pea-souper keeps on. I should say our man considers himself an expert in the art of photography, he has been with us for a decade or more, yet he is at a loss for an explanation of the matter."

"Did you show the photograph to the boy's father, the Admiral?"

"I did not."

Holmes stood and helped himself to one of my cigars from my packet on the mantel. "And you were served coffee in the Library by the maids. The younger boy, William, was with you and the Admiral was not?"

"That is correct, Mr Holmes."

"And Madame Marlowe was, as far as you know, prostrate with grief in her bedroom."

"Exactly."

"You had posted one of your constables outside the death room?" Holmes asked.

"I had. I sent the other outside to look for signs of forced entry at the back of the villa."

Holmes sighed. "That is unfortunate, but never mind. This is all quite intriguing, Inspector. I should certainly like to – what?"

Lestrade shook his head. "You've not heard the half of it, Mr Holmes. Not a particle of the most amazing part of the story."

Holmes folded himself back into his chair and beamed at Lestrade.

"I had confirmed on my arrival at the Admiral's house that a servant was despatched to the telegraph office soon after the body was discovered, and a doctor had been sent for," Lestrade continued. "The doctor summoned was a family friend, Doctor Conan Doyle. He had not arrived by mid-afternoon, and I began to be concerned."

"Doctor Conan Doyle?" I asked. "He has been of great help to me in the publishing of my jottings."

Inspector Lestrade frowned and wrote a couple of lines in his notebook.

"We had reporters gathered at the gate by then, shouting questions at the servants," he continued. "How they sniffed the matter out in the fog, I do not know."

Holmes smiled.

Lestrade looked up. "Well, yes, I do know. The story came from the desk sergeant at the police station in Brompton, as it often does."

He shrugged. "I was shocked to discover, on enquiry, that Doctor Doyle lives on the South Coast at Southsea, he had been invited for dinner and he was not expected until early evening!

"I decided I could not in conscience wait for Doctor Doyle, and the boy's death would have to be certified as soon as possible. I ordered one of the constables to take the train and a cab to the mortuary and bring back the coroner with a mortuary van.

"My man turned up two hours later with the van, but no coroner. The poor chap had fallen into an open manhole in the fog on his way to work, and he was at home being nursed. His assistants were busy with the Drag from the Thames (always a good turnout of bodies, sirs, in a thick fog, what with drunks and carriages falling into the water and pedestrians stumbling off the steps of the landings). I therefore gave orders for the body to be brought out on a sheet and put into the back of the van for transfer to the mortuary."

"Had rigour mortis set in?" I asked.

"I did not notice, Doctor, for at that point, as the body was carried through the hall, Madame Marlowe emerged from a doorway. As you might imagine, she was distraught. The knife handle was clearly visible protruding from the face of the corpse, and the sheet was soaked with blood. We had a devil of a time calming her sufficiently to let us continue our work. I left one constable outside the door of the death room and set out with the other for the mortuary."

Lestrade mopped his brow with a handkerchief, and I prescribed a brandy and soda that was gratefully received. He drained the glass and continued.

"We edged our way across Town through the brown murk, frequently stopping as the constable ranged ahead to find a path with his lantern. We made more progress when we found a group of link boys with flaming torches outside a pub. They saw us the rest of the way for tuppence each, and we reached the mortuary at about three-thirty. The constable and I had a quiet smoke in the lobby as a pair of attendants fetched the body. You can imagine my astonishment when the attendants returned—"

"—without a body!" Holmes said, clapping his hands with delight. "Extraordinary, Inspector. I must say there is never a dull moment when Inspector Lestrade is on the case. I have said that a thousand times, have I not, Watson?"

I supressed a chuckle at Holmes' gleeful expression.

Lestrade was a broken man, pallid-faced and drooping. "I'll be the laughing stock of the Force," he said wearily. "The copper who mislaid the *corpus delecti*, the chap whose cadaver escaped from custody. I can only think the link boys took it for a ghoulish prank."

"You are certain the man was dead?" I asked.

Lestrade shook his head. "Nobody could have survived that wound, Doctor. On that I would stake my life and the tattered remains of my reputation. The room was aswim with blood, and the corpse dead white, completely drained."

"Exsanguinated," I corrected.

Lestrade stood. "The body was missing – not a single trace was left. I'll have to report to the Yard before I return to the scene. Is there anything that occurs to you, Mr Holmes? Any line of enquiry that might be fruitful?"

"There was no note? No suicide note?"

"No, sir. It would be a strong-minded man who could commit self-murder in such a fashion, with a dagger to the eye. I did not think suicide at all likely."

Holmes stood and shook the inspector's hand. "I have five distinct solutions in mind, Inspector, but I can say no more until I have visited the locus of the mystery in Brompton and met the *dramatis personae*. May we keep these photographs for a while? I shall be sure to return them."

Lestrade nodded disconsolately, and I showed him downstairs and out to his carriage. The November evening was cold and, even directly under the lamppost, the light was but a blob of flickering yellow in the murk.

"We're in for a bad 'un, Doctor," Lestrade said, looking around and tapping the side of his nose. "A right bad old London particular. It'll be black as the coal-hole for another day or two."

He lit the hanging oil lamp in his carriage. "And I'll tell you one more thing my nose tells me, Doctor. There are more things in Heaven and Earth than are thought of in detective work. I am seldom led astray by my nose."

The inspector's carriage moved off at the trot and was swallowed by the fog, leaving me in noxious, Cimmerian blackness. I hurried back inside the house and upstairs to the cosy warmth of our sitting room.

I found Holmes dressed in his overcoat and scarf, putting on his gloves. "Come Watson, get yourself ready. You'll need to pack your evening clothes. We'll take a four-wheeler, and Billy will buy torches. There's a stall outside the station on bad days like this. The boy can lead our way to Brompton."

"I've been thinking, Holmes," I said as our cab crept along at walking pace following the glimmer of Billy's lamp.

"Good for you, old chap."

"It's odd, don't you think? Where did all the blood Lestrade described escape from? The wound, terrible as it must have been, was stoppered by the dagger. Whence then did the blood pour from in such quantities? The dead do not bleed."

Holmes nodded. "That is a very interesting observation."

"There may have been another wound," I suggested. "The body was not examined by a medical man."

We reached the Old Brompton Road with fog swirling around the windows of our carriage, irritating my nasal passages and causing a bitter, sooty taste in my mouth.

Admiral Marlowe's villa was set back by a small front garden. Servants with flaming torches met us at the gate and led us up a garden path and a set of steps to a portico under which the butler received us in the glare of two hanging gas lamps.

He was a stooped elderly man, narrow-faced and with receding grey hair. His features were drawn and his face pale in the lamp light. He introduced himself, led Holmes and me into a marble-floored hall and directed Billy to the servant's quarters.

"You found your young master's body and sounded the alarm," Holmes said as he was relieved of his overcoat, hat and stick by a footman.

Frazer bowed acknowledgement of the fact. He seemed too overcome with grief to speak further.

"Show us to Admiral Marlowe," Holmes ordered.

We crossed the hall to a set of double-doors. Frazer knocked, flung the doors open and announced us in a cracked voice.

The room was a library. Tall walnut bookshelves stocked with leather-bound volumes lined the walls and stood in alcoves on either side of a finely carved wooden fireplace and mantel.

A tall, middle-aged gentleman with grey mutton-chop whiskers and wearing a black frock coat sat by the fire reading a magazine. I thought it an odd occupation for a father who had just lost a son, but in my experience, people reacted to tragedy in remarkably different ways, and I did not expect a senior royal naval officer to readily show his grief. The man dropped his magazine as we were announced by the butler, and he stood to greet us.

Holmes darted forward. "Admiral Sir James Marlowe? I am pleased to introduce Doctor Watson, my friend and colleague. I am Sherlock Holmes, the consulting detective."

The admiral had, as I had surmised, mastered his emotions to such a degree he was able to smile a welcome, shake hands and invite us to sit by the fire while Frazer provided refreshments.

"This is a fine room," I said, to ease the conversation along.

"Thank you, Doctor. Much of the house is modern, built in the fifties, but I reconstructed elements from my house in Portsmouth that had to be demolished due to subsidence and woodworm. The panelling here and the whole of the bedroom wing is Elizabethan. We steeped the wood in a stream near Chester known for its insecticidal qualities and had the panels reassembled here. The plasterwork was done by a firm in Stratford-upon-Avon who have expertise in the old methods of construction."

He stood in front of the fireplace and looked at his watch. "We will begin the séance at eight. With this infernal fog, I expect guests will have started out early, like yourselves, so we might sustain the inner man with sherry and tidbits at seven here in the Library, if that suits? Our tennis court outside is naptha lit, but I cannot recommend outdoor exercise in the present weather.

"A brisk nor-westerly in the early hours will whisk the noxious fumes away and give us a bright day tomorrow. Meanwhile, perhaps I could persuade you to join Doyle and me for a game of billiards, when the doctor turns up."

I looked from the admiral to Holmes in astonishment. The old gentleman must be senile, I decided. He did not know, could not absorb or had forgotten his eldest son had been murdered that day or, perhaps worse, had committed the terrible sin of self-murder. The ravaged face of the butler as he handed me a whisky in his shaking hand suggested he at least had a hold on reality.

Holmes picked up a silver-framed photograph from a side table. It showed the admiral, his wife and his two sons: one was in his late-teens, the other a young man.

"Your sons make a fine-looking pair if I may say so, Admiral," he said. "The older boy in particular is handsome."

"Christopher," Admiral Marlowe said with a smile.

"The younger boy is what, about sixteen? He gazes at his brother with awe."

"Seventeen now and almost as tall as Christopher. William looks up to his brother; for years he followed him around like a puppy, and he was devastated when Christopher went up to Cambridge. Christopher is two years older, a prize-winning athlete and scholar; it is natural that William should look up to him."

"William does not share his brother's gifts?"

"His looks and passions, yes; his athletic and mental prowess, no."

A strangled sob came from where Frazer stood by the drinks cabinet.

"Do you have any idea how your eldest son was killed, Admiral?" Holmes asked.

"I say, Holmes—" I half-rose to admonish my friend. His abrupt question was harsh in the extreme.

"I have no idea," Admiral Marlowe said mildly. "But the matter will soon be cleared up."

"I very much hope so," Holmes said, adjusting his cravat. "And I appreciate your confidence in my abilities."

"Eh? No, no, I do not mean by you." The admiral smiled. "I shall simply ask Kit what happened."

"Kit? Is he your younger son?" I asked.

The admiral shook his head. "No, I mean my elder boy, Christopher. Kit is his nickname. We will talk to him later in the evening."

The door opened, and the admiral strode across the room and welcomed another guest.

"This is Mr Ludworth," Admiral Marlowe said as he led a man in a dark suit and holding a bowler to us. We shook hands, and I noticed Mr Ludworth had the hard palms and callused fingers of a working man. Holmes nodded to Mr Ludworth from his chair in his lazy fashion.

"It is with the aid of Mr Ludworth's kind offices we will contact Kit," the admiral said. "He is the medium through whom we earth-bound mortals may communicate with beings on the Higher Plane."

He nodded for Frazer to show Mr Ludworth out, and he returned to his place in front of the fire.

"Ludworth is a railway signalman on the London, Chatham and Dover line. He will not join us at table, of course. I have arranged for him to take his supper with Frazer and the housekeeper in the kitchen."

Holmes and I exchanged looks that the admiral intercepted.

"You may smile, gentlemen, but Ludworth is well-connected on the Celestial Plane. He is a nodding acquaintance of Plato and Emperor Septimus Severus and is on intimate terms with Joan of Arc."

I frowned. "You don't mean—"

"I mean nothing of that sort, Doctor Watson," the admiral said sternly. "Signalman Ludworth is a married man with a wife and six children. He would not think of sundering his marriage vows on even the loftiest planes of the Spirit – especially with a foreign person."

The door of the Library opened once more, and we stood as an elderly lady clad in black entered.

"May I present my wife?" Admiral Marlowe said heavily. "Lady Elizabeth."

She did not wait for introductions. "You are detectives, I presume. You should know my son is a bright and beautiful boy with the prospect of a glittering life before him. He is about to marry a girl from a good, one might say grand, family and enter upon his vocation as a naval officer. Kit would never bring shame on his family." She turned imperiously and stalked from the room.

"Kit was to join the Navy and marry Lady Elisham, of the Shropshire Elisham-Camberleys," the admiral said in a dull tone. "With his commander's permission." He smiled a wan smile. "The commander of the boy's cruiser is Captain Elisham-Camberley, his future father-in-law, so permission was to a degree assured."

He put down his glass. "You will excuse me, gentlemen. I must see to my wife. She is perturbed."

Admiral Marlowe hurried out, leaving the Library door open.

"I say, Holmes, what an extraordinary state of affairs!" I slumped into my chair.

Holmes took a cigarette from a case on the mantel and lit it with a spill. "The matter is not devoid of challenges."

He strode to the bookshelves and prowled them, running his finger along the spines.

"What are you looking for, Holmes?"

"Christopher Marlowe. The poet and dramatist of the time of Queen Elizabeth. Perhaps there is an index."

"There is no need." A tall boy in school uniform had appeared at the door. "I can show you our Marlowe books and papers. We have an extensive collection of his writings, and many books about him and his work. The collection is my brother's."

"You must be William," I said. "Christopher's younger brother." The resemblance between the boy before me and the young man in the family photograph was even more remarkable in the flesh than I had suspected from the picture.

"Will and Kit, sir. We don't answer to those other names. The portrait on the far wall is Kit Marlowe the poet, aged twenty-one."

I examined the painting; the face and clothing were those of the spectre in Lestrade's photograph.

"Will, then," said Holmes. "Could you find me a short biographical sketch of the Elizabethan Kit Marlowe and then perhaps you would convey us to your brother's bedroom?"

Holmes paused at the threshold of Kit's bedroom. He glared through the open door and turned to the white-faced police constable on guard. "Why did you allow this, Constable? The blood has been mopped away, the carpet taken up and the floorboards washed and flogged dry. Were you not charged to secure the scene of the crime?"

"That Scotland Yard inspector took the body away sir, and I thought we was done. Then the housekeeper offered me a nice bit of lamb for me dinner in the kitchen downstairs. I had no idea—"

"Very well." Holmes turned to me. "Come in with me and close the door behind you. We shall see if any traces have been overlooked by the scrubbers. Turn up the gas, will you?"

Holmes stood in the centre of the room and surveyed the dark wood panelling, the four-poster bed and the few other items of furniture: a marble-topped washstand, a wardrobe and a hat stand. What I had thought from Lestrade's images to be a collection of paintings on one wall were photographs of Kit and his friends, presumably taken at Cambridge.

"Quick work for a grieving household, don't you think?" said Holmes. "I should have liked to have seen the earthly remains of the victim or at least the debris left behind. But perhaps higher-level manifestations will available for inspection at the séance."

He pointed to a space in front of the fireplace. "No chair." He flung open the doors of the wardrobe. "A few suits, hats, cravats and ties and a line of empty hangers."

Holmes examined the wood panelling with his magnifying glass. "Sound the walls on the other side, would you, my dear fellow? We are looking for a secret cabinet in which a man might hide."

"A priest's hole?"

"Exactly."

An hour or so later, I admitted defeat. "It's nearly seven, Holmes, and we have found nothing. We will need to change our clothes."

Holmes stood back from the panelling. "Very well, either I am wrong, or we are dealing with a clever devil, perhaps with the master himself." He took down one of the framed photographs from the wall, opened the frame and removed the photograph.

"I say, old man, don't you think—"

"Hush. It is in a good cause."

"The younger brother had an offhand manner," I suggested. "For someone who idolises his brother, young Will is strangely unaffected by his death."

Holmes considered. "You saw Will wears two rings, one a brilliant on his left little finger, the other a signet, and an amethyst pendant hangs from his watch chain. Yet in the police photographs of his brother's body I see no rings and no chain. Would the older brother be less gaudy than the younger? Would he not wear a watch?"

A bedroom was allocated to us to change into evening clothes. We used the lavatory and bath facilities at the end of the corridor, changed and were conducted downstairs by a footman. We met Will on the landing, looking splendid in the newly fashionable, short, tail-less dinner jacket.

"Is there any means of communication between your brother's room and any other? Your own, for example," Holmes asked him.

"We should have found it if there were," the boy answered. "We have lived in the same rooms since we moved here."

"May we see?"

"Certainly."

Will led us to the room next to the dead room and unlocked the door. His room was identical to his brother's, with the same furniture, except that a small sofa and a wicker rocking chair stood on either side of the fireplace, and every surface was heaped with sports and photography equipment, model ships, toys, paintings and piles of magazines.

As in the brother's room, one wall was covered with framed photographs. Holmes pointed to one. "This is Christopher in his rooms at Corpus Christi."

"Yes, with friends."

"You are the photographer, I suppose."

"I visited Kit in Cambridge whenever I could get away from school."

"Your brother also has a wall of photographs," Holmes said, "but you can see from the spaces that several are missing. Have you any idea where they might be?"

"Perhaps he took them to college. They will be shipped back here with his things in due course."

Holmes nodded. "No doubt. You are a photographer. May I ask you a technical question?"

Will shrugged. "I am no expert, sir, but I will try to answer you."

"If you were requested to create an exact facsimile of this photograph, how would you go about it?"

Holmes handed the boy Lestrade's picture of the ghost of Marlowe standing over the corpse of his brother.

"You mean, how would I fake the ghost image?"

"Is it a fake?"

"If I try to recreate it by non-spectral means, then I suppose the resulting print must be."

Holmes smiled. "That's what I thought you meant."

"As I said, I am no expert, but the combination of two images into one is simple enough; getting it to look real, or perhaps unreal in this case, is more difficult." Will smiled at Holmes and handed him the photograph. "Or so I imagine."

"I saw no photographs on your wall of you," Holmes said.

"The camera lens is kinder to Kit than to me." Will glanced at his watch. "We should be getting down. Father is a stickler for punctuality."

Holmes nodded. "That's a fine Hunter. Did your brother wear a similar watch?"

"His is a magnificent antique Breguet, Mr Holmes, given to him by my father. It belonged to my great-great-grandfather, Admiral Grenville Marlowe. He carried it at the Battle of Trafalgar."

We followed Will out into the corridor, and he locked his room with a key on his watch chain.

"You must be looking forward to leaving school and joining the social whirl at college," Holmes said as we trooped downstairs. I winced; his voice oozed false bonhomie. "I expect you hope to make as splendid a match as your brother did."

"I shall marry the lady suggested to me by my father, sir," Will replied in a sombre tone.

Frazer announced us at the door of the Library, and Will slipped away to join the admiral.

A tall, heavyset young man advanced towards us, and I recognised him as Doctor Doyle, the Southsea physician. We shook hands. Doctor Doyle had the firm grip of the keen cricketer, golfer and footballer I knew he him to be.

"May I present, Mr Sherlock Holmes, Doctor?"

"Mr Holmes needs no introduction, Doctor Watson," Doyle said, shaking Holmes' hand. "I might claim to be a follower of yours, sir, through the agency of the Police Gazette and my contacts on the Force in Portsmouth." He lowered his voice to a murmur. "The Maypole kidnapping and the matter of the two sailors in Rye made quite a stir at the time."

"Trifling affairs, Doctor Doyle," Holmes said, straightening his cravat. "Maypole hid his child at his sister's house, cried out the boy was kidnapped and hoped for outpourings of public charity. The sailors were brothers; their elongated earlobes and spatulate toes were proof of that."

"And what of Brighton, Mr Holmes?" Doctor Doyle asked. "The dismemberment."

"And what of Brompton, Doctor Doyle?" Holmes replied. "The stabbing?"

"A sad case," Doctor Doyle said, shaking his head. "We shall doubtless know more from Kit later this evening."

"How well did you know the boy, Doctor?" Holmes asked.

"Very well, I am his godfather."

"How would you describe his character?"

Doctor Doyle considered. "He is strong-minded, even wilful. He caused his father a good deal of trouble when he was at school. There was talk of putting him into a military academy, but it came to nothing. Admiral Marlowe dotes on the boy, and his son gets his way."

"Was he a likeable boy?" Holmes asked.

"Oh yes, he is a charmer. And one mustn't discount his looks; he uses them to his advantage. His brother Will is almost as tall as Kit, but he expends less energy on being amiable. In a few months we'll not be able to tell them apart despite their age difference."

"If Kit had lived," said Holmes.

"Yes, of course. I have not had time to adjust to the boy's passing."

"Will was in awe of his older brother when he was a child?"

"Naturally," Doctor Doyle replied. "Kit was a golden youth and the boys were very close. I suppose they may have drifted a little apart in recent years. I imagine that Kit became involved with a new set at college."

Holmes leaned towards Doctor Doyle. "I should tell you something, Doctor, in the strictest confidence." He described Lestrade's decision to take the body to the mortuary and the extraordinary matter of its disappearance.

Doctor Doyle listened impassively. "How intriguing," he said. He pursed his lips. "I gather you discount the theory the link boys took the cadaver for a jape, and you consider the body removed itself from the van by its own agency. You do not think the van was followed, and the corpse abducted by others?"

"To what end?" asked Holmes. "It would be strange thing to kidnap a corpse."

Doctor Doyle nodded. "The matter is most intriguing. It's Admiral Marlowe's good fortune he has you on the case, Mr Holmes. If it can be proven the poor boy's body disappeared without trace while in police custody, it will open new lines of inquiry in certain Spiritualist circles. I very much look forward to hearing your conclusions, sir. Oh, there is Mr Crown. I thought he might not show up in this disgusting weather. I must introduce you to him; he is a facsimilist."

Doctor Doyle strode across the room to greet a thin, sallow man in gold-rimmed glasses.

"This is inconceivable, Holmes," I murmured. "We are attending a party on the evening of the death of the eldest son of Admiral Marlowe, and only Lady Marlowe and the butler seem in the slightest perturbed. The boy's corpse is hardly cooled, wherever it may be, and the guests here are chatting about the foul weather. It's extraordinary."

"The photographs missing from Kit's room must have been compromising to the plot," Holmes said fiercely. "And where are his rings and other jewellery? He was not wearing his watch when he was killed; that is a most instructive point."

"His box hasn't come down from Cambridge yet," I said. "We understand it is still at the college."

"No sane man ships a valuable watch in a trunk, Watson, particularly not an antique Breguet. And you saw the twinkle in Doyle's eye when I told him of the disappearance of the corpse? We are being played, my friend. I taste the hook in my mouth."

"May I present Mr Crown, the handwriting expert?" Doctor Doyle said, joining us again in the company of the new guest.

"I suppose I am a facsimilist foremost," Mr Crown said after the introductions. "I am often called in to verify the authenticity of legal and literary documents, handwriting, that is. But my interests lie elsewhere, in literature."

"Do you know much of Elizabethan literature, sir?" I asked. "The works of Christopher Marlowe, for example?"

"He was a contemporary of the Shakespeare entity and one of the university wits, along with Green, Nashe, Lodge and others."

I frowned. "The Shakespeare entity, Mr Crown?"

"Naturally, Doctor. No one with any knowledge – any true knowledge – of the Elizabethan period would entertain the fantastic notion Shakespeare's plays were written by a glover's son from Stratford, one who received a rudimentary education at a local school and did not attend university. The so-called Shakespeare plays are the product of Christopher Marlowe's genius; it is a statistical certainty, gentlemen. I could tell you tales of Marlowe's use of the apostrophe that would dissolve any sceptical thought you might harbour on the matter. And Marlowe himself confirmed his authorship through Mr Ludworth, so there can be no gainsay."

He bent forward and continued in a hushed tone. "At this time I cannot give full details of my methods, but in confidence I may tell you gentlemen my investigative technique is based on counting the frequency of certain words in a document. We all have our favourite words, Doctor. It is a fundamental fact of writing."

"And what is the boy doing in London in November? Michaelmas term is not over," Holmes said softly.

Mr Crown raised his eyebrows. "I beg your pardon?"

Frazer offered us a tray of drinks.

"I am sorry, sir," said Holmes. "I was thinking aloud. Have you any idea who might have killed Christopher?"

Mr Crown took a glass of whisky from the tray and leaned towards us once more. "I understand from Admiral

Marlowe," he said, "that the police inspector who first examined the body this morning, an Inspector Lestrange, maintains the culprit in ninety percent of such cases is a disaffected servant."

The butler started like a hare, gulped and moved away.

"Watson," Holmes said, "I am feeling rather hot and flushed. I will step outside for a moment for a breath of air. Would you be so kind as to accompany me?"

I took my friend's arm and ushered him towards the door.

"You'll get no fresh air outside this night," Mr Crown said, shaking his head.

Billy waited beside the back door of the house with a pair of lanterns. He handed one to me, and I followed him and Holmes outside and along the wall of the villa to the bedroom wing. The fog was thick and filthy brown in the lamplight, and I held my handkerchief over my mouth.

"We must start with the obvious premise the photograph showing Christopher with the ghost of Marlowe the poet has been tampered with," said Holmes. "Who had the motive, opportunity and expertise to create the fake?"

"Perhaps Frazer did it to give his grieving master hope his son survived in the Hereafter?" I suggested. "Lestrade said the butler carried the equipment for his young masters on their photographic excursions and helped them in the dark room. Perhaps he picked up a basic knowledge of photography."

"That is a possibility, but unless the police photographer was tricked into not noticing the manipulation of the prints when he was developing and printing them, then the exchange must have been effected when he was having coffee with Lestrade and the younger son."

"That exonerates Will."

Holmes nodded. "Whoever did it over-egged his pudding. And where are Kit's things? You noticed the rocking chair, I am sure, Watson."

"In the photograph of Kit's rooms at college, yes. And there is one in his brother's bedroom upstairs."

"It's the same chair, bearing identical scratches and wear marks on the arms. The chair was returned to London from Kit's rooms at Cambridge. Kit didn't tuck it under his arm as he boarded the train home. No, I would wager a guinea to a ha'penny the rocking chair was sent home with his trunk and other belongings. They are stored somewhere in this house if they have not been sent ahead."

"To the Astral Plane?"

Holmes stopped and examined the flower bed in the light of our lamps. "I would also pledge an oath," he said, "that nobody has loitered on the soil under Kit's window recently, apart from the portly police constable sent by Lestrade to view the ground. This is, as Lestrade would put it, an 'inside job'."

He turned to Billy. "What of the servants?"

"They're keeping mum, sir. They weren't happy being ragged and suspected by Inspector Lestrade, and they're laughing up their sleeves the famous Scotland Yard man, Mr Sherlock Holmes, can't solve the case. I've explained we are a private firm, but they won't be told."

"Never mind, Billy. What is the general feeling in the Servants' Hall towards the brothers?"

"I say, Holmes," I said. "Servants' gossip! Have we stooped so low?"

Holmes sighed. "My dear fellow, that is why I brought Billy – to catch the gossip and gauge the feeling among the servants. Well, Billy?"

"Master Will is well enough liked, though he has a reputation for cruel jokes and rough talk."

"And Kit?"

"Hard to say, Mr Holmes. The housemaids swoon on his looks and go pink, and the men sneer. No tears for the young master downstairs, sir, except from Mr Frazer."

"Was there any talk of Kit and a particular maid?"

"Holmes," I remonstrated. "You go too far."

Billy shook his head. "Not much chance of that, sirs."

Holmes smiled an enigmatic smile.

"I say, gentlemen," Will called from his window high above us. "The séance will begin in five minutes. Father is calling for you."

We slipped into two empty seats between Doctor Doyle and Mr Crown at a round table in the Library. On the other side, Admiral Marlowe and Mr Ludworth, the medium, completed the circle. Frazer doused all but a single oil lamp behind Mr Ludworth, and he lowered the flame until the medium was in a faint halo of light and the men opposite me were barely visible, silhouetted in the red glow from the fireplace.

The Admiral frowned at his watch, at Holmes and then at me before he opened the proceedings, addressing us directly. "You gentlemen, who do not know me well, are no doubt surprised at the equanimity with which I face the tragedy that has struck our house. You must know it is my belief that my beautiful boy has ascended from this Earthly Plane to a higher sphere of existence, the Divine."

He leaned forward and placed his palms flat on the table. "In other words," he said matter-of-factly, "I maintain that Kit is still my son, and whatever has happened, he always will be."

He sighed. "We need to cast aside the negative aspects of this modern world and accept aid and instruction from the Ascended Masters whose mission is to bring the Great Wisdom to us. We must help them restore the Golden Age of Mankind that will allow all true believers to join their loved ones on the Astral Plane in unalloyed rapture."

Admiral Marlowe smiled across the table at the railway signalman who sat in the centre seat. "I very much look forward to Mr Ludworth's being gathered; he has immense influence on the Other Side. I have given him a detailed set of instructions to be carried out on his passing, and through his agency I confidently expect to establish a firm channel of communication between the Earthly and Celestial Spheres. That will shake a few complacent dovecots in the Movement, believe you me."

Mr Ludworth looked pale, I thought, as the admiral contemplated his death with such sincere enthusiasm.

"As to the manner of Kit's passing over, the dagger and so forth, we must recall Earthly blemishes are not carried to the other side: the astral plane is perfect. As is my son." The admiral regarded us, one-by-one with a stern expression, and nodded to Mr Ludworth.

"Right," the signalman said in a strong, matter-of-fact tone. "We will now join hands and spend a moment in meditation while I summon the spirit charged with the reception of new wanderers on the Celestial Plane. I believe General Gordon is on duty this month." He lowered his head almost to the table top.

I reluctantly laid my left hand on the table where it touched the tips of Holmes' fingers, and then did the same with Mr Crown on my right.

Mr Ludworth lifted his head. "Well," he said in a high, querulous voice, "what do you want?"

"We wish to speak to Christopher Marlowe of Trafalgar House, Brompton," the admiral said. "He went across this morning."

"I don't have time for such nonsense," Mr Ludworth said in the same shrill tone. "This is the busy season."

"Oh," Admiral Marlowe said in an abashed tone.

"Is that General 'China' Gordon, of Khartoum fame?" Holmes asked in the silence that followed.

"I am he. What of it?"

"I would like to express my admiration for your services to the Crown, sir. My friend Doctor Watson and I contributed a guinea each to a fund to set up a statue of you in a suitable location in the capital."

"A guinea, you say?"

"Each."

The voice sighed. "I'll see what I can do."

We waited in silence for the medium to speak again. A clock ticking on the mantel and the soft breathing of the gentlemen around the table were the only audible sounds. A sudden flare of light came from my left as Holmes lit a cigar, and in the flicker of the match I saw a figure in the alcove behind Mr Ludworth's chair. The dim figure wore an Elizabethan doublet and feathered hat, and I recognised him from the portrait on the wall. He smiled a faint smile.

"Good Lord, Holmes," I exclaimed. "He is Christopher Marlowe."

"Oh, my dear, dear boy," the admiral sobbed.

The figure swept off its hat and bowed but did not speak.

"Who did it, Kit?" Mr Crown cried in a fervour. "Who murdered you?"

The spectre swept its arm across the occupants of the room and seemed about to settle on someone when the door opened, and light streamed in from the hall.

"I do beg your pardon," said Lestrade. "My constable let me in, and I couldn't find anyone."

I turned back to the alcove, but the spectre was no more, and Holmes was gone. I was astonished to see in the light from the hall that my fingers touched, not Holmes' hand, but Doctor Doyle's.

Doyle beamed at me. "A very successful séance, Doctor. I shall write it up in my notes."

I sat with Lestrade and Holmes in the Library as the Admiral led his other guests in to the Dining Room for supper.

"I chased Marlowe through the open door into the room next door," Holmes said. "It was in darkness, and he knew the layout. I didn't, and I came to grief against a side table and smashed a potted aspidistra. Marlowe escaped into the bowels of the house."

"I found myself touching hands with Doctor Doyle," I said sharply.

Holmes shrugged. "An old Spiritualist ruse. The medium joins the hands of his neighbours to each other rather than to him. He is then free to wave scarves, blow trumpets, tickle his neighbours' noses or light a cigar, as he pleases. I let you both grope across the table until you joined hands, thinking it was with me."

"I was fooled," I said, with something close to a pout.

Holmes shrugged a Continental shrug. "Now, let's summarise what we know. The Michaelmas term at Cambridge finishes in December, but young Kit Marlowe came home in early November."

"You think he was rusticated?" I asked. I turned to the inspector. "Sent home for a time as a punishment."

"No, he was sent down. Remember that all his belongings and furniture are supposedly on the way home."

"Expelled," I explained for Lestrade's benefit.

"The question is, for what?" Holmes continued. "It must have been something very serious, not just because of the University's heavy punishment, but because the consequences of the matter were too dreadful for young Marlowe to face, at least in the Earthly Sphere."

"Are you moving towards the horrible conclusion that the boy killed himself?" I asked.

"No," said Holmes. He handed me the photograph he had taken from the wall of Kit's room. It showed Kit with a group of his male friends sprawled on a lawn, laughing and drinking champagne. Another boy sat apart, looking away from the group.

"Is that Will?" I handed the image to Lestrade.

"I believe so," said Holmes. "Will saw his brother as a young god, better than him in every respect. He thought himself to be flawed and pedestrian by comparison – even ugly. Look how he turns from the camera. Kit left the family home a year ago for Cambridge, where he made new friends and established a new pattern of life, free even from his father's light discipline. Will visited Cambridge regularly, but he cannot have been as close to his brother as he was before. He now had rivals for Kit's affection. We know how easily awe and love turn to disdain and hate."

"Jealousy? Revenge for a slight?" I suggested

"You cite two of the most common motives for murder, Watson. However, before we make any rash judgement, let's investigate Inspector Lestrade's theory."

"Mr Holmes?" Lestrade asked with a frown.

"Let's see if the butler did it."

"Kit was always a determined, wilful boy," Frazer said. He sat at his table in his sitting room on the top floor of the villa and stared into his glass of Madeira.

Holmes sat with him on the only other chair, and Lestrade and I stood behind them. Framed photographs of Kit lined the walls and I discreetly drew Holmes' attention to one showing the boy dressed as his Elizabethan namesake.

"Kit would brook no criticism," Frazer continued, shaking his head. "He would accept no rules. But he was a charmer when he wanted to be, and he always got his way."

"By all accounts Kit had a compelling character," Holmes suggested. "He must have accumulated friends and admirers at the University."

Frazer nodded. "More than was good for him, that's my opinion. He was unused to authority, sirs, and easily led astray."

"His father is remarkably tolerant for a high-ranking naval officer," I suggested.

"The Admiral is much caught up with spiritual matters, sir. And young Kit could do no wrong in his eyes."

"And Will?"

The butler's eyes narrowed. "A schemer. You never know where you are with Master Will. He likes to play games, and show us up – the servants, I mean. He's more his mother's boy than his father's, is young Will."

Holmes nodded as if Frazer had confirmed his observations. "Well then, Frazer?" Holmes asked softly.

Frazer slammed his fist on the table. "Yes, I admit it. I did it, sirs," he said, tears streaming down his face. "I could bear the young master's calumny no longer. I stuck a dagger in his – oh sirs."

"Good Lord, Frazer," Holmes said in exasperation. He looked up at me and Lestrade and rolled his eyes.

"Come you now," he continued in a benign tone as he poured Frazer another glass of wine. "I don't believe you for an instant. You were captivated by Christopher; you would never have harmed him. You were not a party to murder. Why was the boy sent down?"

Frazer's face took on a bleary, cunning look. "A connection with a town girl, as I understand the matter, sir."

"She is in a certain condition," I suggested.

He nodded. "Six months gone and naming young Kit as the father."

"What does the Admiral know of the affair?"

Frazer hung his head. "I cannot speak of that, sirs."

"And Madame Marlowe?"

Frazer drained his glass and reached with a trembling hand for the bottle.

"Come," said Holmes, standing. "Let's visit Will. It is time for a great reckoning in a little room, as Shakespeare, or perhaps the Marlowe-Entity put it."

Holmes murmured into the inspector's ear as we descended the staircase from the servants' quarters, and I reflected on what I had heard.

Kit had fathered a child with a doxy from the town, and he was sent home in disgrace, his hopes of a Royal Naval career lost, and his prospects of a grand marriage dimmed. Was the boy's shame so insupportable that he lost his reason and committed self-murder? Or was Will, consumed with jealousy and unable to endure the fall of his idol and the blow to the family honour, responsible for the fatal blow?

We knocked on the door of Will's room and heard the click as he unlocked it. Will peered out and held up his oil lamp. "Gentlemen?"

"A word, if you don't mind," said Holmes.

The boy opened the door and stood aside to let us in. He wore his night attire. Holmes smiled at me and nodded to the bedclothes spread back on the bed and the cane rocking chair that gently oscillated.

Holmes took the lamp from Will and examined the panelling on the walls.

"You did not join the guests for supper?" I asked the boy.

"I had already eaten, and I was tired."

Will, Lestrade and I watched in silence as Holmes rapped the panelling with his knuckle, peered along the cracks between the panels and at last shook his head, sighed and stood in front of Will.

"I know everything," he said. "This is your only chance to admit what you did. I will promise that if you do so, the police will take no action in the matter, and we will treat it as a childish jape. Is that right, Inspector?"

Lestrade nodded, somewhat reluctantly I thought.

"The inspector is nodding," Holmes said loudly. I frowned in confusion, caught Will's eye, and I am afraid we both stifled grins.

There was a long silence.

"Fetch your constables with crowbars, inspector," Holmes cried. "We'll have the panelling off!"

He swung to a soft sound as a section of brickwork at the side of the fireplace slid out and a young man in a nightgown and cap stepped into the bedroom.

He offered his hand. "How do you do, Mr Holmes? I am Kit Marlowe."

Holmes stepped past him, ignoring the boy's outstretched hand. He held up the lamp, whipped out his magnifying glass and examined the sliding door.

"Extraordinary," he muttered. "It must be the work of Owen." He turned to me. "Nicholas Owen, a Jesuit lay brother, made the finest hiding places for Catholic priests during the repressions. Queen Elizabeth's Protestant pursuivants, or priest-catchers, would raid suspected Catholic houses and look for secret chapels or hiding places into which a priest could run when there was an alarm. I would wager many of Owen's secret nooks have been long forgotten and will remain unknown for generations to come."

"We found the hiding place when we moved here," said Will. "When the workmen reassembled the wood panels from our old house, they revealed two concealed doors made of wood faced with brick, and a thin space between them, just big enough for a man to crouch. We chipped out the plaster and made a secret passage between our bedrooms."

Kit laughed. "We would appear and reappear in each other's rooms at will. It drove Frazer to distraction."

Holmes settled himself in the rocking chair and lit a cigar. "The butler substituted the ghost photograph for one of the police photos."

"We had a plate ready made with the ghost," said Kit. "Frazer made a new double-exposure print and substituted it for the policeman's print."

"It's a simple technique – a child, or even a servant could do it," Will said, winking at his brother.

"The dead body ploy was your invention," Holmes said to Will. "You borrowed the prop dagger and blood from your drama class. I saw from a photograph on your wall that this term's play at your school was the Shakespeare Entity's Scottish Play."

"Will played Lady Macbeth," Kit said. He frowned. "I thought he overdid the blood."

"It worked well enough," his brother countered. "Anyway, I expected we'd only have to fool the local constable from the station. We thought he'd run off for help, and the body would disappear while he was gone. If he left a guard on the door, we'd use the secret passage."

"We did not expect the Inspector to post a guard in the open door," said Kit. "I couldn't move. It was damp, and I got the cramps."

"The blood," said Holmes, "is why you did not wear your watch."

"It is a *Breuget*, sir," Kit answered, "and delicately balanced. We thought such details would not be noticed by the local constable. We did not expect the great Sherlock Holmes to be involved in the case."

"A charming thought, young man, but you had never heard of me before today," said Holmes.

The boy smiled. "Your fame has not quite reached Cambridge, sir, or at least it has not reached Corpus Christi College."

Holmes set the rocking chair moving. "You jumped out of the mortuary van."

"At the front gate. I then slipped upstairs by the back staircase and hid in Will's room until the séance."

"It was a blaggard thing to do," said Lestrade, banging his fist into his palm. "You gave me and the constable a proper turn. If I had not made a promise with Mr Holmes, I'd have you both up before the assizes for false statements and wasting police time."

The boys looked down at their toes, patently unrepentant.

"Was it you or your brother who played the ghost?" I asked.

The boys smiled at each other and said nothing.

"You were sent down for an alliance with a lady from the town," said Holmes.

"Something like that," Kit said with a sly smile. "They called it an 'improper liaison'."

"Your mother is distraught," I said, frowning at Kit.

"She is easily disturbed, sirs. It will pass. She is upset about Cambridge."

"And the Shropshire Elisham-Camberleys," Will added with a grin. "And the censure of Society, of course."

Holmes pursed his lips. "You are both aware the story of the pregnant shop girl, which I do not for a moment believe, will do you no harm in Society. The feeling will be the University has been unnecessarily harsh. You may return after a year or so and go about your occasions – and there are other universities."

"Why?" I asked, shaking my head in exasperation. "Why go to all this trouble? Why not quietly disappear abroad? It is the usual thing in such cases."

"Exactly, Doctor," Kit said. "My brother and I have no intention of doing the usual thing. Life must be lived to the utmost, and not in a bourgeois astral heaven or in a draughty manor house in Shropshire. We livened up a dull, foggy, November evening, did we not?"

He made a low bow with a wide Elizabethan flourish of his nightcap. "If there is nothing else, gentlemen, I should retire to my room and get some sleep. I am on the Boat Train to Holland in the morning."

I stepped out onto the portico and took a deep breath. "The fog's lifted, thank goodness."

Holmes joined me, with Billy and Lestrade. "The admiral's nor'west wind."

"Did the admiral and Lady Marlowe know?" I asked Holmes. "And what about Conan Doyle and the other chap? Were they party to the boys' charade?"

Holmes shrugged. "The admiral's wits were deranged by his favourite son's shameful departure from Cambridge and the end of his hopes for a career in the Royal Navy. His wife was devastated by the social consequences of his expulsion. Admiral and Mrs Marlowe retreated from reality, she into her room and he onto a higher plane. Doctor Doyle may have thought it medically advisable to go along with the fiction and humour an old friend. The facsimilist is of no interest or consequence."

Holmes offered his cigar case. "According to the biography I glanced through, the original Marlowe was murdered by a dagger in the eye in an argument with a waiter over the reckoning, the bill. Or perhaps he faked his death and escaped to the Continent to avoid a charge of atheism. The boys re-enacted both scenes."

"My missing corpse wasn't a corpse at all," said Lestrade. "I thank goodness for that at least; I've been going mad as a hatter thinking about it."

"And I am glad you met Doctor Doyle, Holmes," I said as we settled in Inspector Lestrade's four-wheeler and set off for home. "He has promised to show me a paper he wrote on syphilis – we are wholly in agreement on the agency of syphilitic degeneration of the nerves, and the characteristic *tabes dorsalis* lesions on infected bones."

Holmes coughed. I looked up and saw Inspector Lestrade and Billy looking pale.

"Doctor Doyle is a literary man, like myself," I continued, turning back to Holmes. "He is thinking of writing a historical novel set in seventeenth century. And he has kindly offered to act as our literary agent if and when we decide to publish further case notes. I thought we might make a start with the Indian affair I have in draft. Doctor Doyle will help with the editing."

Holmes smiled. "In years to come, my dear friend, I expect that a learned society will exist dedicated to the proposition the Watson Entity's works could not have been written by Doctor John Watson of 221b, Baker Street, and instead they were the work of another, perhaps the learned Doctor Arthur Conan Doyle, of Southsea."

I blinked at my friend and returned a rather uncertain smile.

THE SKULL OF KOHADA KOHEIJI

I stepped from a hansom at the door of my lodgings at 221b Baker Street and fished in my pocket for my key. It was a bright, sunny day at the end of April, and my mood was buoyant.

I found the key in my waistcoat pocket with a single penny. I flicked the coin to a little girl who stood by the lamppost outside our door selling tiny bunches of violets. She caught the coin deftly and returned a gap-toothed grin. I smiled back, and I hummed to myself one of the strange melodies I had heard during the morning as I inserted my key in the front door.

The door opened as was about to unlock it, and Mrs Hudson stood in front of me, stern-faced and holding our pageboy, Billy, by the collar. Our maid, Bessie, stood behind them looking anxious.

"Oh, Doctor, here you are at last, sir, thank goodness," Mrs Hudson said. "We waited as long as we could, but he's puffed up now like I don't know what."

"I see," I said, as I slipped past her into the hall. "Is there any chance of coffee?"

"Doctor!"

I sighed and turned.

"Billy won't be told. He wants a 'second opinion' from you, Doctor." Mrs Hudson turned to Billy. "Open up!" She pinched the boy's arm, and he opened his mouth. "Wider," she ordered. "There, Doctor, you can see plain as toast. It's got to come out, will he or won't he."

I stepped back out into the street and angled Billy's chin to the sunlight. I grimaced. "Sorry, old chap, I'm afraid Mrs Hudson is right, that tooth is absolutely ripe, and your cheek is puffed up like a balloon."

"It'll drop out in a few days, sir, like the others."

I shook my head. "It might go nasty, then where will you be, eh? I'd have to take off the top of your head to let the steam out."

"Can't you pull it, Doctor?" Billy pleaded.

I backed towards the door. "No, no, Doctor Grant's the expert; he'll have it out in two shakes of a lamb's tail." I pursed my lips. "Or perhaps three."

Mrs Hudson led the disconsolate boy away, his head drooping and feet dragging.

"Wait, wait," I called, and I handed Mrs Hudson a two-shilling piece. "Here's for a cab and toffees on the way back."

I stepped into the hall, humming my odd tune. I beamed at Bessie, but from her glum expression she too seemed down in the dumps. "Cheer up, my dear, it's a jolly, bright, fine day, and all is moderately right with this corner of the world. Coffee, if you please."

I handed her a package. "On the kitchen table, for Mrs Hudson. And this is for you." I gave Bessie a tiny lacquered box. "You can keep whatnots in it."

She beamed at me and curtseyed. "We've tea brewing, Doctor."

"Very well, tea will do." I almost took the stairs two at a time, but saner counsels prevailed. My old war wound had been quiescent for months and I aimed to keep it subdued until the chills of winter inevitably woke it.

I opened the door to the sitting room I shared with my friend Sherlock Holmes and instantly stepped back with my hand over my mouth, coughing and spluttering. The room was a perfect fug of tobacco smoke. I fanned the door for a moment, then groped my way across to the windows and flung them open. The draught expelled the smoke in a cloud that must have alarmed our neighbours.

"Good afternoon, Watson," Holmes said from his chair in front of the empty grate where he sat in his old dressing gown surrounded by crumpled newspapers, his legs tucked under him.

He waved his pipe in greeting. "I see the entente between our dear Queen and the Japanese Mikado still prevails."

"Eh? What do you mean?" I said, planting myself in my usual chair and feigning confusion as Holmes played his mind game.

Bessie appeared at the door with tea. She sniffed the air, coughed pointedly and placed the tray on our dining table.

"Bessie," Holmes said. "Watson wonders how I know he is returned from a visit to a particular place this morning.

Can you see anything in his dress or deportment that might afford you any clues?" He winked at me and puffed on his pipe as Bessie scrutinised me intently.

"I say, Holmes," I remonstrated, reddening and looking down at my toes.

"I can tell the Doctor went to the Japanese Village in Humphrey's Hall," Bessie said. She smiled a superior smile at Holmes and flounced out, giggling into her pinafore.

Holmes stood and avoided my eyes as he returned his pipe to the rack.

"Bessie got you there, Holmes; a veritable hit." I chuckled at my friend's discomfiture. "I told Mrs Hudson this morning I was going to the Japanese Exhibition and suggested she should not wait luncheon as I might be late. I gave Bessie an intricate little box and had her place a package containing a bamboo ladle on the kitchen table as an offering to Mrs Hudson. Presents for you and Billy will come by messenger."

I held up the guidebook I had purchased and showed Holmes the back page.

THE JAPANESE NATIVE VILLAGE

(PROMOTED BY T BUHICROSAN)
ERECTED AND PEOPLED EXCLUSIVELY BY NATIVES OF
JAPAN
(MALES AND FEMALES)
WHO WILL ILLUSTRATE THE MANNERS, CUSTOMS AND ART
INDUSTRIES OF THEIR COUNTRY

CLAD IN THEIR NATIONAL AND PICTURESQUE COSTUMES.

FIVE O'CLOCK TEA IN THE JAPANESE TEA HOUSE

A MILITARY BAND AT INTERVALS

ADMISSION ONE SHILLING

Holmes glanced at the pamphlet, wrapped himself again in his dressing gown and flopped back into his chair, blowing a stream of tobacco smoke across the room.

I sat in my usual chair by the empty grate and sipped my tea in an utterly relaxed mood as I recalled my pleasant and informative morning.

"I'm sorry you weren't with me today, Holmes. The Japanese Village in Knightsbridge is said to be perfectly authentic, and it certainly looked so to me. I watched craftsmen making all sorts of fine and unusual objects, including a delicate guitar or banjo I particularly liked, but the fellow would not give me a price. He played a haunting melody on the instrument in keys unfamiliar to me."

"You hummed the tune as you came through the door," Holmes said with a smile. "That was one of the indications I used to deduce where you had spent the morning."

I took a puff on my pipe. "I might take up the banjo. What do you think?"

"The other indications were obvious," Holmes said. "The guidebook sticking out of your pocket—"

Our doorbell rang, and I heaved myself out of my chair. "That will be the messenger with my parcels."

A knock came at the sitting-room door, and Bessie opened it wide.

A strange figure stood in the doorway. He was of a swarthy complexion, tall, well-built, verging on corpulent and with brown slightly slanted eyes. He was draped in a magnificent yellow and crimson robe cinched with a purple sash, a *kimono*, as I remembered from my guidebook. Below the hem of his gown he wore split-toed, white stockings and wooden sandals.

The gentleman bowed, and I tried to imitate his action; it was more difficult than it looked.

"Good afternoon," our visitor said in an accent tinged with the Orient. "I am Tannaker Buhicrosan, the promoter of the Japanese Village exhibition that one of you gentlemen, Doctor Watson, I believe, was kind enough to patronise this morning."

I bowed again, making a better job of it, I thought. "I am he, and this is my friend Mr Sherlock Holmes, the consulting detective."

Holmes acknowledged our visitor's low bow with a languid wave of his pipe.

"Do take a seat on the sofa," I suggested.

Mr Buhicrosan stepped into the room, revealing a slight teenaged boy behind him who wore a sober, grey version of the wide-sleeved *kimono*, and carried several brown-paper-wrapped packages. The boy bowed deeply, and I copied him.

Mr Buhicrosan snapped something in Japanese, and the boy followed him inside, closed the door, laid his parcels on the carpet next to the sofa and knelt beside them.

"Tea?" I suggested.

"Mr Buhicrosan might prefer to let us know the purpose of his visit before we go on," Holmes said.

"I will do so, Mr Holmes," Mr Buhicrosan said as he settled himself on our sofa. "I admit I am at my wits' end. I was in the Village office conversing with Mr Cornelius Tarrant when I received Doctor Watson's card and his request to purchase certain items from the exhibition. As a rule, we do not accept purchases, except a few bamboo keepsakes on offer in our lobby, as our purpose is altruistic rather than commercial."

Mr Buhicrosan smoothed the folds of his robe. "Our objective is to introduce Japanese culture to the people of Great Britain and to promote understanding between our two great empires. My salary as director is diverted to a fund set up by my dear wife, Ruth (who is Japanese) with the aim of spreading the Word of Christ in the Empire of Japan."

He smiled. "In fact, tea would be most welcome, Doctor, or coffee, for preference."

I stepped around the Japanese boy and called down the stairs to Bessie. She gave me a dubious look from the hall below where she was polishing the hat rack, and I heaved an impatient sigh.

Mrs Hudson was away on her mission of mercy with Billy, and as Bessie's previous attempts with the coffee grinder had not been crowned with success, I was obliged to go down to the kitchen and prepare the brew myself.

"It is simple, Bessie," I explained for the tenth or twelfth time as I roasted the beans. "Watch and learn."

I followed her up the stairs as she carried the coffee tray, and I found Holmes and Mr Buhicrosan leaning across the dining table stabbing their fingers at an open page in Holmes' atlas and in a heated discussion on a subject that eluded me. Bessie and I stepped around the kneeling boy, and I removed an aspidistra plant from an occasional table and made room for her to place the tray.

"Coffee, gentlemen?" I offered.

Holmes and Mr Buhicrosan returned to their chairs, smiling and obviously well pleased with each other.

"As I said earlier," Mr Buhicrosan said, accepting coffee and biscuits, "I was in consultation with my business associate Mr Tarrant, the well-known dealer in Japanese artefacts, when Doctor Watson's request to buy certain items was made known to me. Such requests, even from the Highest in the Land, are invariable refused."

Mr Buhicrosan took a sip of his coffee. I squirmed inwardly. I had no idea I had transgressed in attempting to buy the articles.

"Mr Tarrant," Mr Buhicrosan continued, "informed me that Doctor Watson was a friend and companion of Mr Sherlock Holmes who I knew had unmasked a plot by a rival import agency that would have seen the end of Mr Tarrant's business."

Holmes nodded demurely and sipped his coffee.

"Mr Tarrant suggested I should avail myself of the opportunity Doctor Watson's presence offered and make my predicament known to Mr Holmes through his agency." Mr Buhicrosan turned to me. "I instantly sent word your purchases were to be approved, Doctor Watson."

I bowed again, feeling embarrassed and confused.

"By the time I had dressed in suitable attire to meet Doctor Watson," Mr Buhicrosan indicated his kimono, "he was away in a hansom."

He chuckled. "As you can see, I am neither slim nor lithe, and I had to wait for a four-wheeler. It is an inconvenient fact of life in the metropolis that, despite explicit hire-carriage regulations, some cab drivers do not care to carry a conspicuously dressed foreigner. I found myself in an altercation with one such fellow just outside the Sun Music Hall – the building next to the Village. I almost resorted to fisticuffs. I am a practitioner of the *Ju Jitsu*."

I heard a soft snort and I frowned at the kneeling Japanese boy. My glance met his, and I thought I detected a hint of amusement in his wide-set, almond eyes before he looked coyly down again.

"Perhaps your young companion would like some refreshment, Mr Buhicrosan?" I asked. "And would he not prefer to sit at our dining table? His present position looks most uncomfortable."

Mr Buhicrosan snapped something at the boy who answered in a low voice.

"He is content," said Mr Buhicrosan.

"Perhaps you might like to come to the crux of your problem?" Holmes said.

"It is a matter of ghosts, Mr Holmes. My Japanese Village is infected with them."

Holmes sighed and gave me a despairing look Mr Buhicrosan intercepted. He held up his hands. "I know what you are thinking, Mr Holmes. You have an enviable reputation as a supremely rational man: as the paragon of reason. I ask you to act in the matter on the advice of trusted friends and I trespass on your valuable time with extreme reluctance. As to ghosts, I can only say the soil over which this apparition appeared is not that of England, where such things as demons and spectres are no doubt the province of fools and children, but literally the soil of Japan, where ghouls are commonplace. I freighted several tons of earth from Niigata in Japan to Knightsbridge here in London to make the troupe feel more at home."

I smiled inwardly. Mr Buhicrosan was not only an accomplished showman, he was clearly a skilled negotiator. He had taken exactly the right line with Holmes. My friend was not as immune to flattery as he thought himself to be, and Mr Buhicrosan had delivered an effective dose.

I peeked at Holmes and saw he had put his elbows on the arms of his chair, steepled his fingers and pursed his lips. He smiled and reached into the coal scuttle where, for an unaccountable reason, he sometimes stored his cigars.

"Have a cigar, Mr Buhicrosan," he offered, and I knew he was hooked.

Mr Buhicrosan took one, and he and Holmes cut and lit their cigars, filling the room with a fragrant aroma.

"I shall not trespass on your time for long, sirs," Mr Buhicrosan said. "I have to arrange accommodation for my people for tonight as they refuse to sleep in the Village until the ghost or ghosts are exorcised. The temple monks will preside over a ceremony for that purpose at ten thirty this evening, after the exhibition closes."

He took a puff of his cigar. "Frankly, Mr Holmes, I don't hold out a great deal of hope for the success of the exorcism. I myself incline towards a more rational theory of mind than a spiritual one."

He shook his head. "I found a hotel willing to take my performers if the exorcism fails, but the management was startled by our bathing needs, which are entirely beyond their facilities.

"The Japanese are Roman in their regard for the healing and relaxing powers of very hot water, and they stew themselves in large baths in family, friendly or neighbourly groups. Short of using the Village baths and then leading a hundred Japanese villagers in their night attire through the streets of London to a hotel, I am at a loss for a solution."

He stood and offered his hand, and, unusually, Holmes stood to shake it.

"May I request your company for a late supper, gentlemen, at the Japanese Village at perhaps eleven?" Mr Buhicrosan asked. "I can then give you more details of the infestation, and we may see if the apparition returns."

I ushered Mr Buhicrosan downstairs and outside where a crowd of gawkers and idlers gathered. I ordered Bessie to call George, one of our regular cabbies, from his rank by the station, and she returned with his four-wheeler. I shook Mr Buhicrosan's hand, then had a sudden thought. "Have you not forgotten your boy, sir?"

"No, no," Mr Buhicrosan replied as he clambered into the cab. "I leave Takechan with you to flesh out the particulars of the affair. He can acquaint you with our little ways." He bid me goodbye and instructed the driver to take him to Benson's private hotel.

I returned to our sitting room in some confusion, and again found Holmes poring over his atlas, this time with the Japanese boy.

I leaned over their shoulders and saw the atlas showed Egypt and the Sudan. Holmes pointed to the blue trace of the River Nile. "We were just—"

"No, no, Holmes. Let me guess, I mean deduce, what you and Mr Buhicrosan were conversing about so vehemently and what you are now debating. You are discussing whether the Government should mount a punitive expedition against General Gordon's assassin, the Mad Mahdi of the Sudan!"

The boy laughed, and Holmes smiled. "Not quite, my dear fellow. Mr Buhicrosan, Takeshi and I agree an expedition is necessary as a reprisal and to curb the ambitions of the Mahdi's followers. We were comparing tactical alternatives. Mr Buhicrosan favours a land assault, I contend an attack down the Nile would prove simpler and young Takeshi considers a two-pronged land and river campaign would yield the best results."

"Takeshi?"

Holmes gestured to the Japanese boy who stood, bowed and held out his hand. "My name is Inoue Takeshi," he said in excellent, American-accented English. "I am very pleased to meet you, Doctor Watson."

We shook hands, and Takeshi took three parcels from the table and ceremoniously handed them to me. "With Mr Buhicrosan's compliments, Doctor."

I saw from its shape the first was my gift for Holmes. I passed it to him, and he unwrapped a long, black-lacquered scabbard that held a Japanese Samurai sword. He drew the blade.

"Be careful, old chap," I said. "The edge is razor sharp."

"It is a magnificent gift," Holmes said with a radiant smile.

Takeshi bowed and handed Holmes a sealed letter which he held to the light from the window. "Very high-quality, thick, handmade paper, wax-sealed with a stylized letter F." Holmes regarded Takeshi with raised eyebrows.

"Mr Buhicrosan likes to be called Frank. He is half-Japanese and half-Dutch."

"Very well. The envelope has been sealed three times and opened twice. The sender reopened the envelope, changed the contents, resealed it and then opened it once more. He was in three minds about something." Holmes slit the envelope. "Let's see what sum Mr Buhicrosan decided on."

He took out a letter and a cheque, handed the letter to me and relit his cigar with a match. "What have we to do, Watson?"

"He does not mention me, Holmes, just you. He requests you spend tonight on the Japanese Village grounds in Humphrey's Hall to determine whether the ghost is real (I expect he means in the unreal sense) or the result of a human agency."

Holmes glanced at the cheque. "A hundred guineas. I imagine Mr Buhicrosan wrote a cheque for fifty pounds, then a hundred and finally, remembering gentlemen deal in guineas, he reopened the envelope and substituted this cheque."

Takeshi clapped his hands.

"A hundred guineas for one night's work, Holmes," I said with an avaricious smile. "It is a significant sum. Our gas bill alone last month was—"

"But, Watson, consider; my metier is the solving of criminal enterprises, not hunting ghosts. I have my feet firmly on, well, in this case on Mrs Hudson's Axminster carpet. If I agree to act in this matter, particularly after the recent nonsense of vampires, spectres and sibyls, would that not open a Pandora's Box of apparitions and pixies?"

"We can put a note on the front door, Holmes: 'No demons or ghouls, by order of the Management.' Do remember the gas bill, old man."

"Very well, I'll act in the matter if you will second me. I'll need your *shikari* skills."

"I've hunted jackals, but never ghouls. It will be an interesting experience," I suggested.

Holmes held out his hand, and I wrung it with the greatest fellow feeling as Takeshi clapped his hands again and laughed aloud.

"Well then," Holmes said. "We are invited to dinner in the Village and to a night watch for ghouls."

He turned to Takeshi. "Kindly describe the workings of the Japanese Village, its principal personalities and in particular any rivalries or pockets of ill-feeling that may have arisen either between the villagers or between them and the management." He folded himself into his chair. "Begin."

"And the major classes of ghosts and phantasms, if you please," I suggested, settling in my chair, "with their usual manifestations and the measures of extermination, if any, that may be adopted against each class of demon."

Holmes sighed, and I waved an admonitory finger at him. "It's as well to be prepared. We will be on foreign soil."

Takeshi described the layout of the Village and explained the living and working arrangements of its inhabitants. The troupe had been hired mostly from the north-east of Japan. They were contracted for a tour of two years or perhaps three, with a possible extension if the enterprise proved successful.

Most of the villagers were craftsmen foremost, and many were skilled artisans – my banjo maker in particular. Others were performers recruited from travelling shows and provincial theatres, with a few star instrumental and athletic performers from Tokyo, the Japanese capital, and

Yokohama, its principal treaty port. I had seen several conjuring tricks, feats of balance and musical interludes earlier that day.

"How far are the villagers content with their condition?" Holmes asked.

Takeshi was about to answer when, after a soft knock, Billy entered with the afternoon newspapers. His face was bloated, and a handkerchief or napkin was wrapped around his head under his chin and tied with two rabbits' ears. He shambled to the table, placed the papers in front of us, grimaced in pain, mimed not being able to speak, nodded to Takeshi (who smiled back) and retreated to the door.

Holmes sighed. "A performance worthy of the Alhambra Theatre. Give the boy a nip of brandy and we will excuse him duties for the afternoon. He may avoid Mrs Hudson's wrath by hiding in the alcove as he often does when we are out."

I poured brandy sip by sip between Billy's clenched teeth as Takeshi watched with interest. "We do the same with fish," he said, "but we use sake."

We planted Billy on the sofa in the alcove.

"Shoes off," Holmes called. Takeshi bravely removed Billy's shoes, I drew the curtain separating the alcove from the sitting room and we sat back again at the dining table.

Holmes gestured for Takeshi to continue his narrative.

"There are two camps, Mr Holmes," the boy began. "One is reasonably content: we eat Japanese food, live in our own style and are well-paid. The others miss home, hate being indoors out of the sunlight all day and especially detest being gawked at by *gaijin* – foreigners. They also resent restrictions imposed by Mr Buhicrosan on gambling and drinking. And some are afraid, fearful of London and fearful of – other things."

"Ghosts," I suggested, to Holmes' obvious annoyance.

"Perhaps," the boy answered with a slight smile.

Holmes blew a smoke ring across the room. "Do these parties have leaders?"

"The contented group is formed around my father," Takeshi said. "He is a carpenter, and the strongman in the barrel spinning act."

"Oh, I saw that this morning, Holmes," I cried. "A chap lies on his back and juggles a barrel packed with bricks! It was – ahem." The boy looked down at the table, and Holmes gave me a stern glare.

Holmes gestured to the boy. "Go on."

"The other group, numbering no more than twenty, a fifth of our company, is led by Akechi Mitsuharu," Takeshi continued. "He is our sword expert, and he was at one time, and perhaps still is, a Samurai. Mitsuharu-san is a violent man. He gave his oath to complete a two-year contract with the Village, but he is unhappy at being the object of people's stares, he harbours a strong dislike of *gaijin*, foreigners, and he compares our situation to animals in a zoo. He wants Mr Buhicrosan to release him from his bond and let him return home."

Holmes nodded. "Thank you, Takeshi, for a most instructive account of your affairs."

"What of the ghosts?" I asked. Holmes shook his head in seeming despair, but he listened intently as Takeshi described the scene.

"It was last night. Our company were in the second hall where we stage our shows, just after supper. We played *hyaku monogatari*, sirs, the Hundred Stories. We made a ring of candles, and clustered inside the circle. Each of us told a story (a classic ghost tale or something from personal experience), and after each story was told, we snuffed one candle and drank sake. It got darker and darker, you see, and more intense. We Japanese love ghost stories."

He smiled. "One of the stories was of Kohada Koheiji – a man who turns into a snake or serpent (that's common in Japan)."

He smiled another, more tremulous smile. "As the telling of the Kohada story ended, the great temple drum beat three times, although the priests were with us, sharing our mirth. Then the temple gong struck, filling the hall with sound and tremors, and the candles around us flickered. We were fearful, but Mr Buhicrosan called for calm and he led us back into the Village in a crowd. We followed him up the street to the temple. The only light came from the oil lamps hung outside the houses. We approached the temple and gathered before it. Then someone cried out and pointed. Hovering over the roof was a terrible apparition!"

Takeshi was wide-eyed and pale, and I patted his shoulder in a manly gesture of reassurance.

"It was a huge skull," he continued, "the classic image of Kohada Koheiji after his transformation (although this one looked something like Mr Buhicrosan, which isn't common at all). The apparition nodded and grinned down at us over the painted backdrop of Mount Fuji and seemed about to climb over and descend among us. We scattered and ran, some in a panic to huddle in the show hall and others screaming out into the streets.

It was not until the premises had been searched by a police constable with a lamp that we dared re-enter the chamber. Most people gathered their futons and pillows and laid them in the show hall rather than sleep in their houses. Now, although they are willing to fulfil their obligations to the Village during the day, they insist Mr Buhicrosan find alternative sleeping accommodation. That is not easy as we are used to sleeping on mats placed on the floor, and we require daily hot baths."

"Well," I said. "It looks as if we will have our work cut out, Holmes."

He pursed his lips and made no reply.

I smiled at Takeshi. "You speak English very well."

"I spent six years learning English with a missionary in Nagasaki," he answered. "And Mr Buhicrosan engaged a full-time English teacher as we put the show together."

"Mr Buhicrosan calls you Takechan."

"That's like calling someone named 'John' by the nickname 'Johnny'. Or calling a fat gentleman named Mr Buhicrosan by the nickname—"

My frown checked young Takeshi before he could commit an indiscretion. I stood and looked in on Billy in the alcove. I found him wide-awake and listening to our conversation, so I let him up, and to cheer him gave him present, a wooden practice sword.

Holmes and I decided on a walk in the Park, and we left Billy standing feet apart in the sitting room being instructed in the art of Japanese sword fighting by Takeshi. I thought it wise to secrete the real Samurai sword together with the banjo on top of my wardrobe before I joined Holmes on the pavement outside and we set off in companionable silence.

"Well, Holmes," I said as we passed through the Park gates and meandered towards the Serpentine with the usual throng of strollers, "Mr Buhicrosan is not in full control of his people."

"I believe he wanted us to know of dissension in the Village, but not from his lips. He left the boy to explain."

"A section of the troupe wants to go home," I continued, "and they are led by a man of violence. I've read stories of the ferocity of the Samurai sect that beggar belief. They test their swords on passing strangers." I swished an imaginary sword. "There is a verb for that act in the Japanese language."

I took my friend by the arm. "I say, old man, let me stand you a pot of tea at the Japanese Village. We can judge the atmosphere for ourselves before we embark on our mission tonight. It's a short walk; the hall is just by the Albert Gate."

Holmes smiled and nodded assent. "I hope they have the Darjeeling white. It is so much more aromatic than even the first-flush Assam."

Holmes looked down his long nose at the small bowl of green tea on the lacquered tray before him. A charming and beautiful waitress in a bright kimono smiled at me and poured tea into my cup.

"*Arigato*," I ventured, with a glance at the crib in my lap. "Thank you."

She bowed. "*Do itashimashite.*"

"Righto," I agreed, losing my place in the guidebook.

Holmes rolled his eyes.

"As you can see," I said, pointing to a diagram in my book, "the main street of the Village leads to the temple, and both sides of the thoroughfare are lined with shops and houses. Until a day or so ago, the craftsmen and shop people lived above their places of work, but, as we have heard, that is no longer the case since the, ah," I dropped my voice to a whisper, "since the apparition."

I directed Holmes attention to the scene before us and read from the guidebook. "The village comprises a broad street of houses and shops set against a backdrop of painted scenery. The buildings are constructed of bamboo, wood and paper in the traditional manner, with shingled or thatched roofs. There are further rows of smaller shops along one side, with a Buddhist temple and Japanese garden at the end. Individual shops display all manner of manufactures – including pottery, carvings in wood and ivory, toys, fans, cabinets and cloisonné, lacquer-work, textiles, musical instruments and embroidery.

"A second building is used for theatrical performances and displays of martial arts. Both buildings are lit in the daytime by skylights in the roof and at night by Japanese lanterns made of—"

"Enough," Holmes said, pushing his tea bowl away. "Pay the girl and lead me to the temple and the martial arts ring."

I led Holmes along the village street to the temple. According to my guidebook, two priests had accompanied the travellers from Japan, a fact that gave me pause until I read a statement from the projectors that pagan religious ceremonies would be conducted after hours, and there was no intention of proselytising the Japanese cult and causing offence.

We stood before the brightly painted temple building. Holmes ignored the fine woodwork adorning the facade and the magnificent dragon carved on the cornice; instead he peered up at the painted backdrop of Mount Fuji hanging against the wall behind the temple. He stepped onto a wooden platform to take a closer look and a gaudily dressed Japanese gentleman hissed at him and pointed to his shoes. Holmes waved him away, turned and stalked down the street.

I hurried after him and steered him into the next hall, in which various feats of conjuring and physical prowess were exhibited.

I pointed out a lady dressed in a flamboyant kimono and standing on stilt-like wooden shoes who danced to a banjo tune and kept a paper butterfly floating above her head with wafts of air from a pair of fans. Farther into the hall, a booth had been set up not unlike our venerable Punch and Judy shows, and a puppet play was in progress.

Holmes strode to a circular arena in which two men dressed in padded clothes and wicker masks traded cuts with wooden swords identical to the one I had given Billy. The players leapt at one another and struck the torso and head of their opponents with heavy blows.

Holmes turned to me and smiled. *"Kenjutsu* – the 'Method of the Sword'."

I watched as the two combatants lunged and swung at each other, stamping their feet and uttering fearsome war cries. I could discern no pattern of point-scoring, and the referee, resplendent in a pink and yellow kimono, seemed to content himself with high-pitched yelps at random intervals.

The tall fellow on the left had a clear advantage in that he wielded not only a wooden sword, but a wooden dagger. He also had several inches on his opponent and he was much the heavier man.

I frowned. The blows the taller man dealt were applied with an intensity suggesting an intention to hurt and cause injury rather than a sporting spirit. The slighter right-hand man played fair and came up to scratch after each round with such evident pluck I became caught up in the bout and began to cheer his hits.

Several gentlemen in the crowd watching the fight also cheered their favourites, and I was offered 'two-to-one on the midget' by a man in a clergyman's habit beside me.

The referee became agitated and called a sudden halt to the bout, garnering groans and boos from the audience. The fighters bowed to each other, stepped off the platform and removed their helmets and armour.

"Rain stopped play and all bets are off", called a wag. My laugh died in my throat as my eyes locked across the ring with those of the taller swordsman. He cradled his helmet under his arm and gave me a look of absolute hatred. A young Oriental-looking man in a Western suit and bowler pushed through the crowd, leaned towards him, nodded towards me and made a remark I could not hear.

"Come," Holmes said, taking my arm. He led me away, but we turned back when we heard shouts behind us.

The tall swordsman held his wooden sword high and faced the young man in the bowler. He stood white-faced with one hand inside his jacket.

Holmes led me back into the Village exhibition hall. "What a stormy petrel you are, Watson. You stir things up wherever you go."

"I say," I exclaimed, looking past him. "What are you doing here?"

Takeshi and our pageboy stood before us. Billy had removed his bandage, but he pointed to his face and mimed he still couldn't speak. He passed me a packet of toffees. I took one and offered the packet to Holmes, but his attention was still focused on the altercation in the room behind us.

"What are they saying, Takeshi?" he asked.

The boy listened for a few moments. "Akechi Mitsuharu is the tall man in the *Kenjutsu* armour. He is saying rude things to the man in the suit."

"Mr Akechi is the ex-Samurai you described earlier," Holmes said. "The one who wants to go home."

Takeshi nodded.

"He is a violent fellow," I said. "Who is the pale man in the bowler? I do believe he is carrying a firearm in a shoulder holster."

Takeshi looked nervously around us. "I must go. The puppet-master will be looking for me; I am his assistant." He bowed deeply and hurried away.

Holmes, Billy and I made our way to the exit. As we passed through the doors, the pale-faced man in the bowler pushed in front of us, elbowing me aside.

I felt Holmes' grip tighten on my arm. "Do nothing," he murmured, and he continued out loud. "I have heard Japanese food is less than sustaining, Watson. I understand Orientals do not use a great deal of meat, but vegetables and rice make up for the deficiency. Perhaps we might stop somewhere for a hearty chop or a steak to fortify us for our vigil tonight?"

The man in the bowler jumped into a hansom without looking back, and I breathed a sigh of relief. "Who was that fellow?"

"I have no idea, but clearly our case may involve human as well as supernatural agencies and we must be on our guard. Billy, grab that cab."

We stopped at a chophouse in Mayfair, where we took pity on Billy, allowing him a small portion of vegetable soup with soft bread while Holmes and I tackled splendid beefsteaks with roast potatoes. Strangely, the poor boy did not seem much bucked up. We waved pudding away and caught a four-wheeler home to Baker Street.

"Our appointment with Mr Buhicrosan is at eleven," Holmes said as we settled ourselves upstairs. "If the spirit has any sense of duty, it will manifest itself at or around the witching hour of midnight—"

"Tokyo time, Holmes?"

"—so, let us spend the next few hours in quiet contemplation and with a mellow pipe or two."

"I must write up my case notes."

"My dear fellow, you are not thinking of associating my name in the eye of the public with a ghost story? I have my reputation for cold, hard, logical acumen to think of."

"What does your vaunted cold, hard, logical acumen say of the case so far?"

Holmes lit his pipe from a gas burner and slumped back in his chair. I poured us a glass of Madeira each.

"The apparition appeared while the company were in the secondary hall where we saw the *Kenjutsu* and you put Anglo-Japanese relations back a decade or two," Holmes said, "Agreed?"

"To the former proposition, not the latter. But were the villagers counted? Some might have sneaked out."

"That had crossed my mind. Alternatively, other persons who mean ill to the Village may have used trickery to effect the skull apparition. I take it we are as one that no actual ghostly creature appeared however much Japanese soil has been sprinkled about. The Village is in Knightsbridge, not Kyoto."

I nodded reluctantly.

"The company is riven with dissension," he continued. "Some villagers are desperate to return home to their native heath, and the leader of that faction is a volatile character, held fast to his contract by a Samurai oath."

I shuddered as I recalled the venomous look Akechi Mitsuharu had given me. "And the pale-faced man, Holmes? What is his part in the affair?"

Holmes smiled. "I have not the faintest—"

A loud crash startled me, and I was showered with broken glass as something flew across the room and thudded into the wall.

"Down, Watson." Holmes dragged me from my chair and pulled me next to him. We shrank with our backs against the outside wall. Three more missiles came in quick succession, slamming into the wall opposite us.

"This may be the prelude to an attack," Holmes murmured. "Douse the gas, and I will fetch my revolver from my room. Ready?"

I heard a thunder on the stairs and thought our assailants were already in the house and all was lost, but the footsteps pounded past the sitting-room door and up towards the next floor.

"Go," said Holmes. He leapt up and raced into his bedroom. I hauled myself off the carpet and swiftly turned off the gas taps, plunging the room into darkness. I heard footsteps in the corridor, the door was flung open and a slight figure appeared silhouetted against the dim hall light.

"I have him," Holmes said from the open door of his room. He raised his gun, and the figure waved a heavy pistol and squeaked something unintelligible.

"Do not fire, Holmes," I cried, "for God's sake, do not fire."

I helped Mrs Hudson put up the shutters as Bessie swept up the broken window glass.

"I should put you across my knee," I said.

Billy coloured and hung his head. "Which, I fetched your service pistol for you, Doctor, thinking the house was under attack," he answered between clenched teeth. He looked at the shuttered windows and at broken glass littering the carpet. "And it bleedin' was."

"Language," I admonished him. I sighed. "Do we carpet beat the boy or give him a medal, Holmes?"

"Wilful mite," Mrs Hudson said fondly. "Billy dropped his knife and fork (we were in the kitchen having a bite of supper –liver and bacon as tender as you like) when we heard the glass break. He leapt out of the room without a word, peeked into the waiting room, jumped up the stairs and took the Doctor's pistol out of his drawer and ran down to the sitting room with it. He's a hero, what with his bad tooth, Doctor, he's a little hero."

I picked up a heavy lead dart from the carpet. "They used these to break the windows, then they threw in the other blades. Were our attackers Akechi Mitsuharu and his Samurai minions?"

I reached for one of the shiny, silver, star-shaped knives stuck in our sitting-room wall.

Holmes held my arm. "Be careful, they are razor sharp." He took one of my thick leather fishing gloves from my desk, slipped it on and plucked the blade from the wall. It lay glittering in his palm. "Get me down volume M - O of the index, will you, old chap?"

I pulled the heavy scrapbook from the shelf and laid it on the table. Holmes leafed through to 'N'. "Here we are, an article from *The Illustrated London News* of last year: 'Well-versed in the stealthy crafts of war, they use disguise and concealment to get close to their target and loose their weapons.'"

He indicated an illustration of outlandish weapons, climbing aids and mottled clothing designed to conceal the wearer. "These darts and stars arc the weapons of the *Ninja*, the spies and assassins of Japan."

"I saw them from the waiting room window, sir," Billy said. "They was on top of a furniture van passing the house and dressed in black all over."

"You did well," I said, patting the boy on the shoulder.

Holmes looked at his watch and at me. "It's time."

We took a hansom to the Japanese Village, arriving well after ten, the closing time for the exhibition. Takeshi waited at the door, and he ushered us into the Hall and past the houses and shops which, though lit by paper lanterns, were empty of inhabitants.

As we neared the temple, we saw the people of the Village knelt in silent rows before its open doors while two gorgeously dressed priests of their faith performed a ritual to placate their idols. The temple drum sounded, the priests chanted and a cloud of incense drifted across the congregation.

I stopped. "I say, Holmes, I'm not sure we should—"

"Good evening, gentlemen," Mr Buhicrosan said, coming up behind us. "Shall we leave the people to their devotions? I have supper prepared in the garden."

He dismissed Takeshi and escorted us up a narrow side street to a Japanese garden, brightly lit by clusters of tiny paper lamps. A table set with Western-style plates and cutlery stood amid the foliage, and we took our places on dining chairs as a diminutive lady in a flowered kimono bustled out from one of the houses leading a procession of servant girls carrying trays.

Mr Buhicrosan introduced his wife, Ruth, who supervised as the various dishes were laid before us but did not join us for dinner.

I regretted my earlier beefsteak as I struggled to do justice to a fine banquet of delicious and daintily presented Japanese food. To my surprise, we were offered beer as well as wine and sake. The beer, a cool lager produced, according to the bottle labels, by a Dutch concern in Yokohama, formed a very suitable accompaniment for the Japanese dishes. The only sombre notes, in what was a merry gathering, were the frequent chants and mournful drum beats that echoed from the ceremony at the temple.

Mr Buhicrosan was an excellent host, ready with small talk and anecdotes of the exhibition's reception in London. We laughed as he explained that his wrestlers, huge, tubby men in scandalously brief costumes, had been incensed almost to the point of resignation when visitors laughed uproariously at their heroic efforts to heave each other out of the ring.

According to our host, in Japan their exertions would have been greeted with the roars of approval we British reserve for our boxers, pedestrian racers and cyclists.

He told us that Mr Gilbert, the librettist of the famous operetta *HMS Pinafore*, had requested the loan of several female villagers to train the cast of his new Japanese-themed operetta in the art of kimono-wearing and fan flapping. The new piece, tentatively titled *The Mikado*, was to be authentic in every respect.

Mr Buhicrosan's tone hardened as he described attempts by competitors to suborn his performers into joining imitations of the Village in other cities and even abroad. He lowered his voice almost to a whisper as he talked about efforts to sabotage his exhibition, and he showed us a notice he had placed in *The Times* earlier in the year.

ONE THOUSAND POUNDS will be PAID to any person or persons who can prove that any of the inhabitants or employés of the JAPANESE VILLAGE, Albert-gate, Hyde-park, have, since their arrival in England in November last, suffered from smallpox or any other contagious or infectious disease; a false, unfounded, and malicious report being circulated by some evil-disposed person or persons that they have been so afflicted being utterly untrue and without foundation.

"Who do you suspect is behind the plots?" Holmes asked.

Mr Buhicrosan shrugged. "The business rivals I have mentioned, perhaps."

Holmes glanced at me and smiled. "Doctor Watson and I had a visit this evening from black-clad gentlemen who threw these through our windows." Holmes took a handkerchief from his pocket and opened it on the table to reveal a dart and a star blade.

"*Ninja!*" Mr Buhicrosan exclaimed, jumping up. "But no one was hurt? Then it was a warning, otherwise you would be dead."

He subsided into his chair. "My dear sirs, I cannot permit you to proceed further in the matter. You must withdraw; it is too dangerous."

The mournful thumping of the temple drum increased in tempo.

"That is impossible, sir," Holmes said. "The attack may, as you suggest, have been a warning. Alternatively, it may have been a challenge: a glove thrown down, a gauge. You mistake me if you think I will not take up that glove, Mr Buhicrosan."

I thumped the table with my fist. "Hear him!" I said.

"And Doctor Watson, of course," said Holmes. "He is no milksop to be frightened by darts and gentlemen in black."

"Let us hope," Mr Buhicrosan said in a solemn tone, "the only enemy you meet tonight is a ghostly one."

We drank a toast to that, and as we lit our cigars, all went quiet. The exorcism was over.

We stood, and Mr Buhicrosan wrung our hands. "I have to see to my people; they grow daily more restless. Are you sure I cannot persuade you to relinquish your interest the matter? It is most unwise for you to ignore the warning you have been given. The *Ninja* are implacable enemies."

Holmes smiled a more confident smile than I could have mustered and shook his head.

"Would you like me to leave the boy, Takechan, with you?" Mr Buhicrosan offered. "He can interpret as necessary."

"I do not foresee the need to engage in conversation with the skull of Mr Kohada," Holmes observed. "We will be fine, thank you."

We followed Mr Buhicrosan back down the street. The villagers had left, the lanterns had been doused and the few oil lamps outside the deserted temple and shops gave a meagre light enabling us to find our way to the entrance of the hall where we shook hands and said our goodnights.

"One question, if I may," Holmes said. "Is it permitted for me to climb onto the temple roof?"

Mr Buhicrosan gave Holmes an odd look. "Yes, I suppose so, if you remove your footwear and show a proper respect for the building."

"Thank you."

We closed the door behind Mr Buhicrosan and turned towards the Village. I took a paper lantern attached to a bamboo rod from outside one of the houses and lit it to provide us with more light and a little cheer.

Holmes checked his revolver. "We must be prepared for anything, Watson, but I feel the locus of activity will be the temple. The ghost may not come; it may have been expelled by the exorcism, but if it is still 'alive' in any sense, it will want to vaunt itself again at the temple, if only to show its power."

I nodded doubtfully. "Where shall we take post?"

Holmes took another hanging paper lantern from a bracket and we held our lanterns before us as we retraced our steps back up the street, following the line of shops and houses to a building opposite the temple. We found the coil of rope and other articles we had asked to be left for us.

I led the way to the temple with my lantern. Holmes slipped off his shoes, then lit and clipped a dark lantern to his belt. He pulled the rope over his head and shoulders, hoisted himself onto the pediment above the tall, ornate doors and climbed up onto the curved roof using carved wooden idols and curved cornices as hand and footholds.

A beam of light shot out from the roof as Holmes opened the shutter on the lantern. He played the light across the painted scene of Mount Fuji forming the backdrop to that section of the Village.

"What are you looking for, Holmes?"

The lamp went out, and I blinked to recover my night sight as Holmes dropped beside me. "It is nearly midnight. Let's make our stand in the shop opposite and await the arrival of Mr Kohada."

We doused our paper lanterns and settled ourselves on the woven mats covering the floor of the shop. As my night vision improved, I became aware of dozens of dolls of all kinds sitting and standing on the mats and on shelves above me. For a reason I could not fathom, I found their blank stares disconcerting. I was about to make a remark on the phenomenon when Holmes gripped my arm.

I followed his gaze to the temple roof, and above it to the backdrop. As I watched, Mount Fuji seemed to cant to one side as the fabric drooped.

The temple gong clanged, the great drum beat three times and a strong beam of light lit a hideous skull, ten feet high, grinning and leering at us as it peered over the backdrop. It stretched a skeletal arm over the cloth and seemed about to spring to the attack. The drum beat again, and then again, increasing in loudness and tempo to a tremendous crescendo, then it stopped, the light went out, the gong sounded one last lonely clang, and all was still and quiet.

Holmes stood and slowly clapped his hands. "Bravo, Mr Kohada; a creditable performance. The drum work was particularly effective."

I stood and toppled against a wooden pillar as my leg, unused to the uncomfortable position I had been in, gave way. I felt the wind of something pass my face before it lodged in the pillar above me with a thunk. It was a star blade.

Holmes knelt beside me. "Our ghost has strange ways of manifesting itself." Another star skimmed across the street and split the head of a doll on a shelf by my right ear.

"That came from the musical-instrument shop," Holmes whispered. "Let them see we are not toothless. I will start our pheasant and you may bag him."

I sighted on the music shop as Holmes aimed across the street and let off three shots with his revolver. I sensed a slight movement at the open window of the shop and fired, to no discernible effect. I stood and staggered across the doll shop to the doorway to find a better shooting angle and tripped over a black-draped figure crawling across the floor. My pistol dropped from my hand as I fell, and I twisted onto my back and scrabbled for it, then froze.

Above me was the dark outline of a man without a face. He drew a long Samurai sword from a scabbard on his back, raised it high and, about to run me through, crumpled to the ground.

Holmes' silhouette appeared in the doorway behind the body, hefting a heavy wooden mallet. "Bong," he said. "I borrowed one of the gong mallets from the temple."

I picked up my gun, turned the body of my assailant over and lifted the black mask covering the face. "Is that not the pale-faced man who argued with the *Kenjutsu* player?"

Holmes smiled. "Two more to go if they are the same troupe who attacked our house. Billy counted three men on top of the furniture van."

We turned our heads to sounds of a struggle in the toyshop across the street. The structure shook as something or someone crashed around inside. I stood, aimed my revolver and then blinked in astonishment as a severed head in a black mask flew through the paper wall of the shop, bounced on the dusty street and rolled to a halt.

"Two down, one to go," said Holmes, grinning.

A movement caught my eye to the right. A shadow flitted down the street towards the entrance of the hall. I swung my pistol and aimed ahead of my bird, but a tall figure leapt out from behind a pillar, swung his sword in an arc glittering in the light of a hanging oil lamp and the shadow cartwheeled onto the ground.

The tall man moved to the centre of the village street, turned towards us and shouted something in Japanese.

I looked at Holmes; he shrugged.

"Are you addressing us, my dear sir?" I called.

"He says it is safe for you to come out," a tremulous voice called in English. "He has killed the last attacker."

I followed Holmes into the street as young Takeshi appeared from behind the temple trailing a huge kite on strings behind him. We joined the tall man as he wiped blood off his sword on the black suit of the second decapitated *Ninja*. I recognised him as Akechi Mitsuharu, the Samurai swordsman.

"That, I presume," Holmes said, gesturing to the puppet, "is the skull of Kohada Koheiji, the ghost."

Takeshi hung his head.

"You have caused a great deal of trouble to us and to your employer, young man," I said sternly.

"I want to go home to Japan," Takeshi said, streaming tears. "I don't like it here. I want to be with my family and my friends."

Despite my sympathy for his plight, I felt obliged to give the boy a look of stern rebuke.

The Samurai spoke to us, and Takeshi translated. "Mitsuharu-san asks what you are doing here and what business this is of yours?"

"We act for Mr Buhicrosan," Holmes said. "And may I ask what Mr Akechi's role is in the affair, and what he knows of the *Ninja* who attacked us?"

Takeshi translated Holmes' question and Mr Akechi's reply. "Akechi-san says these men are not *Ninja*. He has kept a night guard since the Village was threatened; it was a duty owed to Mr Buhicrosan and the villagers. He discovered the infiltrators were merely *Yakuza*, vile gangsters. Akechi-san says he is a Samurai, and there is no honour in disposing of such vermin, but they must be eradicated. He heard one of the *Yakuza* tell the other that you had killed their leader, and he asks where the body lies."

I pointed to the doll shop, and Mr Akechi loped across the road and disappeared inside. He came out and shouted again.

"Akechi-san chastises you for not making sure of the man," Takeshi said, looking fearfully around us. "He is gone."

He dragged us into a tailor's shop and blew out a hanging oil lamp. We stood in deep shadow.

Akechi strode into the street and called out a challenge. He turned, raised his sword and dagger and called again. We saw a glint of silver and Akechi swayed as a star blade flung from the darkness across the street hummed past him. Another star blade flashed after the first, and there was a clang and sparks flew from Akechi's sword blade as he deflected it. Another flash and a star slashed across Akechi's left arm, and he dropped his dagger and bent to his knees in agony.

"Where is the devil, Holmes? I can't see to shoot!" I said in desperation.

A black-garbed figure emerged from one of the shops and raced towards Akechi screaming a fierce war cry, his sword held high in a two-handed grip. I sighted my pistol, but Holmes laid a hand on my arm. "Mr Akechi would not thank you."

Akechi crouched without moving, his left arm hanging useless, but the instant the *Yakuza* slashed down he dropped to the ground, rolled and swung his sword at his opponent's legs. The *Yakuza* leapt high, and the blow missed.

The swordsmen recovered, stood and faced each other. The *Yakuza* held his sword above his head, two handed. Akechi held his right-handed with the blade aimed straight at his opponent.

The *Ninja* leapt forward, feinted to one side and cut to the other. The blade hissed in a glittering curve and Akechi turned it aside. They traded blow for blow, their sword blades whirling and clashing with clear high notes in a rhythm as strange as the alien music I had heard that morning.

"Mr Akechi is wounded; it is not a fair fight," I said.

"No, no, it is superb," Holmes said in a dreamy voice, "a ballet of death."

"Poppycock," I murmured, but I was as mesmerised as my friend.

Takeshi gasped as Akechi lost his footing and his sword swung high and wide leaving him open and defenceless. The *Yakuza* leapt forward, his blade poised for the killing blow.

He lunged and Akechi shifted his sword to his wounded left hand and struck, point upward. The sword pierced the *Yakuza*'s chest, and he staggered, fell forward, dropped his sword and collapsed to the ground.

Akechi stood, bowed to the corpse, flicked blood from his sword and sheathed it.

I strode across the street and examined his arm under his ripped sleeve. "You are bleeding profusely, sir. You must let me wrap the wound."

Akechi smiled, outwardly calm, but with eyes charged with fierce energy. "*Arigato gozaimas.* Thank you, Doctor."

All was silent in the Hall as I bandaged Mr Akechi's arm. Holmes stood in a trance, doubtless reliving the fight in his mind. There were times, I thought, when Holmes—

"I smell smoke," Takeshi cried. "The *Yakuza* set a fire."

With a whoosh and a soft boom, the music shop disappeared in a sheet of yellow fire. A hot wind staggered me as the thatch on another roof burst into flames. Black smoke roiled across the ceiling of the hall.

Mr Akechi picked up his dagger, slipped it into the scabbard on his belt and raced towards the temple.

Holmes, Takeshi and I stumbled down the street, coughing and spluttering in the thickening smoke. Red and yellow sheets of flame seemed to reach out at us from the tinder-dry shops on either side as they took fire with an enormous rushing, crackling sound.

I turned at the entrance and looked behind us. The painted backdrop was ablaze, Mount Fuji was ringed with fire and glass from the clerestory roof crashed to the floor. The temple was a mass of roaring flames.

As I watched, shielding my face from the heat of the inferno, the ropes holding the great gong to its beam burned through and it fell with a mournful bong. It rolled down the temple steps, wobbled along the street and toppled, quivering.

I followed Holmes and the boy through the Village doors onto the pavement outside, and from fiery Japan into the mild, clear air of Knightsbridge.

The sound of galloping horses and the clang of bells heralded a fire engine that careered around the corner and screeched to a stop against the kerb, its two horses bucking and capering.

Holmes and I stood to one side, lit our cigars and watched as the fireman unrolled hoses, operated steam pumps and shot streams of water through the entrance doors. Clouds of smoke and spark-laden billows poured from the doors and the broken windows let into the roof.

"Well," Holmes said, "the fire will no doubt do away with the ghost of Mr Kohada Koheiji."

Mr Buhicrosan appeared through the smoke.

"I'm terribly sorry, sir," I said, shaking his hand. "I'm very much afraid your Village is destroyed."

"I am relieved to see you uninjured," he replied. He turned to the flaming building. "Yes, it's done with. But we have an invitation to the Berlin International Hygiene Exhibition coming up soon. That will give me time to rebuild here, bigger and better, with working shops selling goods. You will hardly believe the demand for Japanese *bric-à-brac*, Doctor. You would not believe it. I totally underestimated the demand." He shook his head, contemplating his error.

I gave Holmes a slightly bemused look and turned back to Mr Buhicrosan. "Mr Akechi, the swordsman, suggested to us the attack was not by *Ninja* hired by your business rivals, but by—"

"*Yakuza*," Mr Buhicrosan answered softly. "A representative of one of the gangs visited me a week ago. He said our depiction of peasant society in Japan was undignified as it portrayed the Japanese people as backward and uneducated. He said it undermined his organisation's prestige with the people they protect (he means extort from). He threatened violence if we continued the show.

Some of our people have been personally bullied, and others have been offered money to leave and return home."

"Was one of those your swordsman, Mr Akechi?" I asked. "We saw him losing his temper with a pale-faced man. He defeated him in single combat."

Mr Buhicrosan nodded. "Akechi-san considered the approach, the offer of a bribe, as dishonourable, and he reported it to me. He has a fine sense of *bushido*, of Samurai honour."

"What of the *Yakuza* bandits. Will they not strike against your rebuilt village?" I asked.

Mr Buhicrosan smiled. "They are reasonable people on the whole, Doctor. The young man was a firebrand, ha! And he paid the cost. I am thinking of broadening the shareholder base of the Village. The *yakuza* will be more amenable if they have an interest in the project, and their involvement will quell any slight unrest that might arise in the company if we have to extend our engagement for another few months."

"What of Mr Akechi? I hope he escaped the inferno."

Mr Buhicrosan smiled. "He is pleased with himself, having bloodied his blade in so spectacular a fashion. The villagers fete him because he rescued certain important religious objects from the temple and our cashbox, an act of bravery that has endeared him to them. I believe he will stay and display his sword-fighting prowess for the edification of the citizens of Berlin."

"And Takeshi?"

Mr Buhicrosan smiled. "That scamp. It was an excellent puppet the boy made, don't you think? It was forbidding, but Ruth, my estimable wife, saw an absurd resemblance to – well, never mind. We have decided to commission another and include it in our show."

Holmes and I strolled home around the Park towards home, smoking our cigars and enjoying the balmy evening.

"Sun Tzu, the Chinese author of *The Art of War*, counsels pretending inferiority and encouraging the enemy's arrogance," Holmes said, his eyes shining bright in the weak light from the street lamps. "Mr Akechi feigned a severe wound to draw out his opponent. He and the *Yakuza* chief traded nineteen exchanges of cuts. I have never seen anything so beautiful."

I smiled as I took my friend's arm, but I decided that, for the time being, the Samurai sword I had given him might best remain on top of my wardrobe.

THE THIRD MONK

A GHOST STORY

The train slowed, iron wheels rumbling and squealing as we crossed a wooden bridge. I sprang up, lowered the window, and peered out. We were rounding a gentle curve and approaching a rural station.

"We're there," I said. I took a deep breath of the crystal-clear, heather-scented air and was instantly wracked with a spasm of retching coughs.

"Ha," cried my companion.

I turned back into the carriage and reached over his head to retrieve my rod case and Gladstone bag. Holmes sat in a litter of notebooks and newspaper pages.

"You will remember, our host's name is Montague," I said.

"Am I in my dotage, Watson? Do I exhibit signs of decrepitude?"

"Angus Montague." I attempted to gather my friend's belongings, but he batted me away.

"And your connection is —"

"My dear Holmes, as I have explained several times during our journey, Angus and I were doctors together in the Afghan Wars. He removed a Jezail bullet from my arm. It was a delicate operation: the bullet lay against my brachial artery and throbbed with my heartbeat."

I pulled on my greatcoat. "Montague now has a fine practice in Edinburgh. Dunsinon Abbey is his father's country seat."

Holmes sniffed. "I thought you were shot in the leg."

"That was the second Jezail bullet. I took that out myself."

The train jolted to a halt in a cloud of steam.

"You will be affable, won't you, Holmes? You'll enjoy the fishing once you know the ropes."

"You use ropes?"

I ignored his gibe. "The air will do you good. It'll sweep out the dregs of that dreadful fog."

The pea-souper as we left Baker Street for the station that morning was of the kind we used to call a London particular, oily, filthy-brown and stinking. We had to employ linkboys with flaming torches to guide the cab through the fog-shrouded streets.

The only blessing of the foul weather was that it had enabled me to induce Holmes to join me for a short break visiting an old friend in the Lowlands of Scotland.

I opened the carriage door and stepped onto the platform. Holmes pulled on his caped overcoat, clapped on his bowler hat, wrapped a long scarf around his neck and over his nose, and joined me.

"What a view, Holmes," I said. "Look at the lake and the bosky hills beyond, and that icy stream bubbling and tumbling along the valley floor. What a lovely bronze colour are the fading ferns." I took another deep breath of the crystal-clear air.

"Oxygen is a potent poison," Holmes said in a muffled voice as he buttoned his gloves. "You have a sooty smut on your nose."

I dabbed at my nose with my handkerchief, but stopped as a tall man in an open grey overcoat advanced towards us.

"My dear Watson," he said.

"Montague, old friend."

We removed our gloves and shook hands.

"I was very nearly late," said Montague. "Betsy threw a shoe on the road."

"Let me introduce Mr Sherlock Holmes."

Montague held out his hand. "How do you do Mr Holmes? I hope you had a pleasant journey."

"Ten hours and eight minutes from Baker Street," said Holmes, blinking at the vista of lake and forest that lay before us. "With two changes of train."

He sneezed violently, and then again. "My spirit is an urban sprite; it is rarely wise for me to venture far beyond the outer suburbs of London. I was quite at my ease until we passed Watford."

I raised my eyebrows to Montague and smiled a wry smile.

"I am sorry to hear it," he said, replacing his glove. "This way gentlemen."

We followed him through a small gate where a dogcart stood hitched to an elderly bay horse.

"Do you fish—" Montague began. He caught my look and continued in his most solicitous doctor's tone. "I mean, do you care to sit forward or back, Mr Holmes?"

"I always face the future with equanimity," said Holmes. "It is my nature."

Montague helped Holmes up to the front seat and turned to me with a wink. "In that case, Watson and I will turn backwards and wallow in our reminiscences."

The driver clambered up beside Holmes.

"You have your old rod case with you, Watson?" Montague asked jovially as we jogged along. "Do you still use that heartwood fifteen-footer and dry fly?"

"I do."

"I've a pair of split bamboo beauties I got in Edinburgh. Shall we try our luck in the morning?"

"By all means, Montague, and I'll bet you half a guinea my old rod bests your new-fangled bamboos."

He laughed. "It's a wager."

"That's a fine lake," I said, calling over my shoulder. "Look at the way the pale sunshine glitters on the waters. I say, Holmes, is it not scenic?"

Holmes turned to the driver. "What is the name of the lake, my man?"

"We call it the Lake, sir."

Holmes waved a gloved hand at the trees on either side of the path. "And the woodland we are passing through is, I conjecture, the Forest."

"Aye, sir, so it is."

"But the horse is not the Horse; she is Betsy."

The driver looked at him in astonishment and made a sign against the evil eye.

I grinned and nudged Montague with my elbow. "What fine country," I said. "It reminds me of—"

"Afghanistan," Holmes murmured.

"Cornwall," I said firmly.

We followed a gravel driveway along an avenue of noble elms, catching occasional glimpses of a large grey house through breaks in pine tree plantations.

As we drew near Dunsinon Abbey, the path widened, and I twisted in my seat and craned my neck for a clearer view of the facade. The house was long and widespread, obviously the result of building and rebuilding over several centuries. The central and largest part of the building was pillared after the fashion of Palladio. The ivy-shrouded left wing was Romanesque in style, and evidently very old. The right wing continued the pillar and pediment theme of the centre, giving the house a melancholy, unbalanced look.

We stopped under the central covered portico.

"The Abbey," Holmes murmured.

A boy held the horses while McPherson unloaded our luggage.

Montague introduced the butler, Malloch, and ushered us into a high entrance hall. The ceiling was of intricately carved oak, and a fine array of deer heads, antlers, and ancient weapons adorned the oak-panelled walls. A wide, curved wooden staircase stood before us.

"We usually sit down at six," said Montague. "Is that too early for you gentlemen?"

"No, no," I said. "I'm absolutely famished, and so is Holmes. Aren't you, Holmes?"

He grunted something unintelligible as Malloch helped him off with his hat and scarf.

"Well," said Montague. "You'll join me in the Library for a drink when you're settled." He indicated a large double-doored arch to the right.

We followed the butler up two flights of stairs and into a large bedroom. A four-poster bed stood against the wall between two windows that filled the room with fading winter light. A plump sofa, a writing table and chair and a marble-topped, mirrored dressing table completed the furnishings. A gilt-framed painting of a stag at bay hung above the bed, and a stuffed salmon – a prize specimen – was fixed to one wall.

A merry log fire burned in a dog grate set into the left wall.

I strode to the windows and opened them wide. "I say, Holmes, what a delightful prospect. The western sky is shaded in resplendent reds and purples, mirrored in the lake." I turned back to Holmes. "Should you care to take this room, or—"

Holmes had already removed his boots, and he was toasting his feet at the grate and filling his pipe.

"The windows, Watson, if you please."

I closed the windows with rather more firmness than was quite polite.

"Hot water's on its way, sirs," said Malloch, lighting a pair of candles on the mantelpiece. "And the necessary is in this cupboard." He opened the doors of the dressing table to reveal an ample china chamber pot decorated with thistles.

My room across the hallway had a view of the stables.

I went downstairs after my ablutions and found Holmes with Montague in the Library, a large room, comfortably furnished with leather chairs and sofas. The walls were hung with the inevitable stag and deer heads, and a collection of stuffed animals – a badger, wildcat and various eagles – stood on a sideboard. A huge, gloomy painting hung over the fireplace.

"It's by van Honthorst," Montague said, noticing my glance.

"Ah," said Holmes. "Gerrit van Honthorst as he was known in his native Utrecht. He was patronised by Queen Elizabeth of Bohemia, the sister of Charles I, and, as you will doubtless recall, the Electress Palatine."

"It's quite hard to make the picture out, even in daylight," said Montague. "There's a couple of centuries' accumulation of soot. It purports to be a Honthorst copy of 'The Taking of Christ' by one of those Renaissance Italians in the dim, shadowy style that was all the rage then."

"*Chiaroscuro,*" said Holmes, "light and shadow. In Italy, they called Honthorst, Gherardo del Notte for the night-time candlelit subjects he specialised in. He was an incomparable technician, utterly devoid of imagination."

Malloch entered with a tray of glasses. He poured three glasses of sherry from a decanter on the sideboard, passed around a plate of Abernethy biscuits, and left the room.

"We get the boy to give the painting a scrub in spring cleaning week in April," said Montague, breaking the silence that followed Holmes's remark. "It's no so dull for a few months, and then it darkens again. It was collected by my father on the Grand Tour."

"Oh, how remiss of me," I said. "How is Lord Burley?"

"Quite well," said Montague. He turned to Holmes. "My father is somewhat retiring. He spends a good deal of his time in the North Wing with his collections. He does not receive visitors."

"I trust our presence will not discommode his Lordship," Holmes said with a sniff.

"No, no," said Montague. "You are very welcome. Father is much engrossed with his *bonsai*."

Holmes looked at me. "Miniature Japanese trees."

"I know," I said, perhaps a little sharply. "I visited the Japanese exhibition at Humphrey's Hall in '86. You, if you will recall, declined to attend. You were busy with your smelly chemicals."

Holmes whipped out his magnifying glass and peered at a corner of the dark painting. "Indeed, Watson. And the results of that little experiment saved an innocent man from the gallows. This painting is rather interesting—"

I heard a sudden muffled scream and a muddle of voices. The library door burst open and Malloch and a maid half-carried an elderly man into the room. His face was a mask of blood.

"Father!" cried Montague. "My God, what has happened?"

He and I helped Lord Burley to an armchair. "I'm all right," he said in a faint voice. "Don't het yourselves."

"Florrie," Montague said to the maid. "Fetch my medical bag. It's in my study – run, girl."

I stood aside as Montague examined his father's forehead. "Quite a deep cut, Father. You'll need a couple of stitches. Take a look, would you Watson?"

The wound was not very deep, but it was two or three inches long. It bled a great deal as head wounds invariably do.

"What happened?" Montague asked his father.

"Accident: bumped me head on a candle bracket in the cellar. It's just a bruise."

Malloch entered with a bowl of hot water and a pile of towels. The maid followed him with the medical case and I helped Montague clean his father's face and staunch the flow of blood.

The old man's face was pale and drawn. He looked up at his son. "Angus, these gentlemen have the advantage of me."

"I do apologise. Father," said Montague. "This is Mr Sherlock Holmes from London, and my colleague in the Afghan Wars, Dr John Watson."

Montague delved into his doctor's bag and then took me by the arm. He held up the needle and thread. "I say,

Watson, would you mind? I can hardly play the physician with my own father."

I nodded and with Lord Burley's permission, I began to sew up the wound.

"Perhaps a brandy?" Holmes suggested.

"Yes, of course," said Montague. "A dram for his Lordship, Malloch."

Malloch stepped to the Tantalus on a side table and poured a glass of whisky. He handed it to Lord Burley.

"Yes, a dram for his Lordship, of course," said Holmes. "And perhaps—"

"Certainly, sir," Malloch said with a sniff. He gave Holmes a small measure of cognac.

"Now, what really happened?" Montague insisted. "Malloch, where did you find his Lordship?"

"In the cellar, sir. Florrie heard a cry and came to me. I knew at once it was him up to his games again."

"Och, getaway with you, Malloch," said Lord Burley. "They'll think us country bumpkins."

"It was the monk. He it was, and no other," Malloch said firmly.

"Well," said Montague. "You may indeed think us rather quaint, gentlemen. It seems my father was attacked by one of the family ghosts."

"Splendid," said Holmes. He dropped into a wingback chair and leaned forward with interest.

"I say, Holmes," I said stiffly. "Splendid is a bit rich. His Lordship was not injured for your entertainment."

Holmes ignored my remonstrance. He rested his elbows on his knees and steepled his hands. "Pray continue."

"Well," said Montague rather reluctantly. "Father keeps his – I'm not sure what to call it."

"Plant mould," said Malloch.

"Manure," said Montague.

"Shite," said Lord Burley.

"Father keeps his *bonsai* material in one of the cellars under the East Wing," Montague continued. "The East Wing dates from the eleventh century when the abbey really was an abbey."

"What order?" asked Holmes.

"Dominicans, I believe."

"Ha," said Holmes. "The *Domini canes*, the Hounds of the Lord. They wear the black *cappa*, Watson."

"I am aware of that Holmes. I have an aunt in Primrose Hill."

Holmes turned the full force of his deep-seated, razor-keen eyes on me and frowned.

"There is a large Dominican priory between there and Hampstead Heath," I said.

Holmes waved for Montague to continue.

"The under-gardener, who usually went down for the material, gave his notice two weeks ago. The cellar is dark, damp and cold, and I had asked my father to send one of the other servants for the mould, but he would sometimes go himself."

"What religion was the ex-under-gardener?" asked Holmes.

Montague turned to Malloch.

"He was Catholic, sir."

"Note that, Watson," said Holmes.

"We are Kirk, naturally," Montague continued. "Church of Scotland. But my father allows several of the more trusted inside servants to attend the Presbyterian chapel in the village. No notice is taken of the religious affiliations of the garden workers. A practice we may have to rethink, Malloch."

"Indeed, sir."

"And now, if you will excuse me gentlemen," Montague said, "I will take my father to his bed." He and Malloch helped Lord Burley from the room, leaving Holmes and me alone.

Holmes poured himself another cognac. "Did you hear that servant's name, Watson? Florrie. It is a vile diminutive of Florence; a favourite name of housemaids these days. I don't suppose the people of Florence are well pleased their venerable city name is bandied about in such a fashion. I ask you, my dear fellow, would you call your daughter Paris or Basingstoke?"

"You seem to be taking this ineffable twaddle of ghosts seriously, Holmes. I've heard you say that the villains we chase have their feet planted firmly upon the earth. No ghosts need apply. You've said it a hundred times."

"That was in England. Different rules obtain in the North, even the lowland North; they have different postage stamps, bank notes, public holidays and apparitions. Besides, an assault has occurred; it is a demonstrable fact.

And tomorrow is All Hallows Eve, when spirits have licence to range abroad."

Holmes resumed his minute examination of the painting above the fireplace. "Just look at the brushwork here, Watson, eh? You will have instantly noted the *pentimenti*, here and here – where the artist has changed his mind and painted over his previous work. What copyist would bother with that? No, there's more to this than meets the eye."

Dinner was a subdued affair. Holmes was in a reverie of his own, and Lord Burley, although he had graciously joined us for dinner, contributed little to the conversation. Montague and I kept up a somewhat forced exchange on fishing and our plans for an early-morning expedition to a nearby stream.

As we finished our coffee and lit our cigars, Holmes sprang to life. "You said ghosts, Mr Montague? In the plural."

"Aye, Mr Holmes. We have three, all monks."

Holmes grinned. "Watson would be very interested to meet your ghosts, gentlemen, if that could be arranged?"

"With pleasure," said Montague.

Lord Burley muttered under his breath, pulled himself to his feet and bade us goodnight. He was helped from the room by Malloch. As the door closed, we heard a perfectly audible whisper. "We can look after our ain spirits, your Lordship. We need nae English detectives footering about in our business."

We armed ourselves with lanterns from the Gun Room and, with a disgruntled Malloch in the lead, we climbed the stairs to the roof space above the North Wing.

"This is part of the house is twelfth century," said Montague. "The original abbey was built in the 1140s and lasted through to the Dissolution of the Monasteries in the sixteenth. That's when my ancestors acquired the property."

"I gather from my reading," said Holmes, "that acquired would be a polite term for the process."

"Aye," said Montague. "There was considerable violence. The monks were thrown out by King Henry's men, and any who objected were mistreated or slain."

He led us to a corner under the eaves where a great, iron-bound, wooden chest lay. "Here we are."

"This is a cedar linen press," said Malloch, lifting the massive lid with considerable effort. "Brother Wills is its sole inhabitant."

He knocked on the side of the chest. "Are ye there, brother Wills?"

I heard, to my surprise, a faint sound of snoring.

"That's all ye'll get from him," said Malloch with a proprietorial smile. "He's nae trouble at all."

"He's been known to sneeze in a bad winter," added Montague. "And reports suggest he had a bout of hiccups in sixteen twenty-two."

"On," said Holmes, "to the second monk."

Malloch led us down to the ground floor, and through a discreet door into the service corridors of the Abbey. The

THE THIRD MONK · 259

floors were carpeted with worn hemp, and aside from our lamps, the only light came from an occasional low-flamed gas jet on the wall. We came to a place where two corridors intersected.

"This passageway connects the kitchen with the dining room," said Malloch.

A pair of housemaids appeared carrying trays of empty dishes.

"Come here," Malloch ordered. "The gentlemen want to know about Old Francois."

One girl stood looking shyly down at the floor, but the other was bolder and smiled at us. I recognised her as Florrie.

"The second ghost," said Holmes. "Old Francois is it? How does it manifest itself?"

She gave him a puzzled look.

"What does it do?" I asked gently.

Florrie's companion reddened.

"I'm not sure I should say, sir," Florrie said with a faux-demure look. "It isna genteel."

"Och, away with the both of you," said Malloch.

They scurried off, and, as they turned a corner, Florrie looked back and gave me a brazen wink.

"It's like this, gentlemen," said Malloch. "Old Francois lies in wait for the girls coming and going along this passage. He creeps up on them and tickles them behind the knees."

I heard a muffled giggle from farther up the corridor and an earthy snigger.

"The fiend!" I cried.

"Calm yourself, Watson," said Holmes. "I expect the maids avoid this place and use another route."

Malloch shook his head. "No, sir. I cannot rightly say they do."

He pointed down as the heavily stained hemp carpeting. "Soup."

"On, then to the third manifestation," Holmes cried. "Lead on Malloch."

Malloch led us down narrow twisting passageways into the bowels of the Abbey. We stopped before an iron door, and Malloch fumbled with an ancient lock. He heaved the door open, and a waft of chill, musty air escaped from the blackness inside. There was a heavy taint of decay in the air.

"Ah," said Holmes with relish, rubbing his hands together. "This is more like it: dark and dank."

We descended the stairs in a line behind Malloch and I was heartily glad of the light from our lanterns. It grew more and more chill as we descended, and the smell of overripe decay grew stronger.

We reached the bottom and stood in a circle on a floor of worn and uneven flagstones. Water dribbled along the joins of the stone walls, and on the edge of our pool of light was a mound of evil-smelling vegetable matter. I shone my lamp upon it, and the light reflected on shards of white china.

"His Lordship's plant mould," said Malloch. "And his wee Japanese pot."

"What is this third monk's name?" asked Holmes.

"He doesn't have one," answered Montague. "He's relatively recent – sixteenth century – and he's an infrequent visitor. The last note on him was in the accounts for seventeen eighty-eight. Three pence deducted from a servant's wages for a jug broken by the cellar ghost."

A low moan echoed off the walls, as if the mention of the ghost had drawn or awoken him, and a hooded figure appeared in as faint an outline as if it were a mere shadow of starlight; it hovered over the pile of mould, pulled back its hood, and revealed eye sockets of an even deeper blackness. Its features seemed to waver uncertainly between a grin and a grimace. It raised its arms and slowly lifted off its head.

Malloch screamed and darted up the stairs.

Holmes gave me his lantern and slow-clapped his hands. "Bravo," he said. "Any other party tricks?"

A long, deep growl filled the cellar.

"Our friend has indigestion." Holmes sniffed. "These third-class spirits hide in musty cellars, screech at under gardeners, and throw china at elderly earls, hardly marketable accomplishments in the modern age."

An ear-splitting snarl echoed off the cellar walls.

Holmes smiled. "At the Duke of Aosta's *palazzo* in Rome, I was once entertained by the spectre of Cardinal Benicce of Padua on the violin; it played an early baroque solo caprice with demanding pizzicatos for the left hand."

He blew a cloud of cigar smoke at the ghost. "*That* was a haunting. Are you musical at all, Brother?"

The dark figure let out a long gurgling roar, and a shard of china whizzed past my ear.

"Your aim was better this afternoon," Holmes said. He flicked his cigar ash at the apparition, and the ash instantly blew back over me.

"I say, Holmes!" I said crossly.

"Let's go, Watson. I can see nothing of interest here."

Montague led the way up the stairs.

"Good evening to you, Brother," Holmes said, waving an insouciant hand.

A piece of china smashed against the wall beside my head and covered my hair with dust and sharp particles.

"Revenge!" echoed around the chamber.

Holmes paused at the top of the stairs. "Of course," he said conversationally, "if you would care to take tea with Watson and me tomorrow at four o'clock in the Library, we would be delighted to further our acquaintance."

The following morning, after a fine dawn start on the river with Montague, I walked with him up the driveway to the Abbey. His ghillie followed with our catch, and a boy carried our rods and boots.

My friend had seemed somewhat preoccupied during our expedition. "Thank you for an interesting morning and a good catch," I offered. "Honours about even, I would say."

"Indeed," Montague replied. "We had capital sport." He hesitated. "Mr Holmes seems a touch different from the man you describe in your interesting memoirs."

"It was impertinent of him to invite a malignant spirit to tea. I told him it wouldn't do."

"I meant different in a more general sense."

I considered. "Between us, old chap," I answered. "I have had to inject a certain amount of vim into the printed character. And I am obliged to undervalue my own contribution to solving our cases, naturally."

"I suspected as much," Montague said with a smile. "Mr Holmes' interest in that old painting seems quite morbid. It's as if we had a plumber in for the drains and he spent the day admiring the curtains."

We walked around the back of the Abbey and into the gunroom.

"Give the fish to Mrs McKay, Colin," Montague said to the boy. "Then you can clean Dr Watson's fishing tackle. He'll be taking the evening train."

Having been up well before dawn and on the river for a couple of hours, I was famished. I completed my toilet and went downstairs. I found, to my surprise Holmes ensconced in the breakfast room.

"My boots smell of trout," he said. "It is your fault."

I beamed at him.

"Oh, very well, Watson. How did you fare?"

"Eight fine fish."

"Well done, my dear fellow. I had no idea you were such a competent rod and line man."

I examined the chafing dishes. "This porridge looks tasty."

"Wallpaper paste. Moreover, there is no coffee, only tea. The hospitality of the Lowland Scot is not to be relied upon."

At that unfortunate moment, Montague walked in. He either did not hear, or did not choose to hear, Holmes' gibe.

"You had a fine catch, I understand," Holmes said with an impenitent smirk.

"Yes," Montague replied. "And here they are."

Florrie brought in a platter of steaming trout and offered it to me. "Ghillie says you caught yon big, braw one, sir," she whispered. "And you tired after a restless night."

Our eyes met, and I coloured.

The boy, Colin, followed her in with *The Times* on a silver salver.

Holmes snatched the newspaper, then stopped, sniffed and gave the boy a narrow look before snapping open the newspaper.

We sat in the Library at four forty-five with a teapot and plates of sandwiches on a side table beside us. Montague smoked a cigarette and read an illustrated magazine; Holmes again peered at the old painting through his glass. He stood back. "Have you noticed anything peculiar about this painting, Watson?"

I stood with him. "It is very dark."

"Look at Judas' arm."

At first, I could see nothing remarkable; then it struck me. "Why Holmes, is it not too short? Was Iscariot deformed in body as well as in spirit?"

"Your tea is getting cold," Montague said, looking up from his magazine. "And so is Its."

"We cannot expect a twelfth-century cleric to be aware of the fashionable hour for tea," Holmes replied sharply.

As he spoke there was a faint snigger, a shimmer in the air and an almost invisible shadow appeared above the fireplace. "Revenge!" came a squeaky cry, quite different to the booming voice in the cellar.

"Would you care for tea?" Holmes asked. "One lump or two?"

The shadow quivered and darted at the tea table. Montague sprang back as a teacup lifted itself a few inches into the air.

"Not the Spode!" cried an anguished voice from outside the Library door.

The cup clattered back onto its saucer. The wreath of mist seemed to hover unsurely for a moment, then it weaved itself around a miniature tree in a pot on the windowsill.

"Not the *Camillia japonica*!" came a second cry.

A single tiny leaf dropped onto the carpet.

The mist drifted slowly towards the fireplace writhing and twisting. Then, with a faint howl, it disappeared up the chimney.

Holmes consulted his watch. "If we leave now, we might get the six-ten train after all."

Colin drove us to the station in the dogcart.

"I don't quite understand what happened, Holmes."

"It's simple, Watson. Young Colin is the guilty party."

The boy stiffened and went pale; Betsy sensed his agitation and capered nervously.

"He helped cook prepare the fish this morning," said Holmes airily. "Then he polished our boots."

"I meant the Affair of the Third Monk, Holmes."

Holmes shrugged. "The spirit had accumulated enough evanescent ether over a century or so to enable it to manifest itself." He smiled. "Children of a certain sort can pout for considerable periods, but ghosts have just so much evanescent ether and it accumulates very slowly. In inviting the spirit to the Library, I gave it a task that used up all its energies. The phantom had to make its way through twenty feet of solid rock and then the fabric of the Abbey, losing ether all the way. It will be quiescent for another century at least."

"I see," I said. "And who was calling through the keyhole? Another restless spirit?"

"No, and it wasn't a servant. Any competent housemaid or butler would spy with far greater facility. Our eavesdropper was Lord Burley, afraid for his china and plants."

I considered. "And what drew you so often to the painting, Holmes? You took a great interest in it. Is it a fake?"

"I'm afraid so. Lord Burley bought it as a copy of 'The Taking of Christ' by the Dutch master, Van Honthorst, but Honthorst would never have permitted himself to paint that misshapen arm of Judas, or those intertwined sausage fingers of Christ – Honthorst was a master technician."

"So, who was the painter?"

"His Lordship was sold a pup. That painting is an original work by a little-known and little-valued Renaissance hack called Michelangelo Merisi da Caravaggio."

-oOo-

A NOTE ON SOURCES

The Japanese Village

There are surprisingly few sources of information on the Japanese Native Village Exhibition of 1885 – 7, but a couple of internet pages give an outline of the event, and programmes and tickets can be seen on some sites.

Sir Hugh Cortazzi, British ambassador to Japan in the 1980s, wrote a brief, but beautifully illustrated account of the exhibition in 2009. It is available from the Sainsbury Institute for the Study of Japanese Arts and Cultures, 64 The Close, Norwich NR1 4DH, UK for about six pounds.

For more information about the Japanese Native Village and more images please see my website http://kaleidoscopeproductions.co.uk.

Kroomen

"The Kroomen are indispensable in carrying on the commerce and maritime business of the African coast. When a Kroo-boat comes alongside, you may buy the canoe, hire the men at a moment's warning, and retain them in your service for months.

Their object in leaving home, and entering into the service of navigators, is generally to obtain the means of purchasing wives, the number of whom constitutes a man's importance. The sons of 'gentlemen' (for there is such a distinction of rank among them) never labour at home, but do not hesitate to go away, for a year or two, and earn something to take to their families. On the return of these wanderers–not like the prodigal son, but bringing wealth to their kindred–great rejoicings are instituted. A bullock is killed by the head of the family, guns are fired, and two or three days are spent in the performance of various plays and dances. The 'boy' gives all his earnings to his father, and places himself again under the parental authority. The Krooman of maturer age, on his return from an expedition of this kind, buys a wife, or perhaps more than one, and distributes the rest of his accumulated gains among his relatives. In a week, he has nothing left but his wives and his house."

Journal of an African Cruiser, Horatio Bridge USN (1845)

Conan Doyle and Spiritualism

Sherlock Holmes is the arch rationalist, but his creator claimed to speak with the dead.

The creator of the super-logical detective was a medical man steeped in empirical reasoning during his studies at Edinburgh University, but Conan Doyle was fascinated from his mid-twenties on by Spiritualism, early experiments in thought transference and healing through mesmerism. He spent the last years of his life writing and lecturing on those subjects.

Doyle was introduced to Spiritualism between 1885 and 1888 when he was invited to the home of one of his patients, General Drayson, a teacher at Greenwich Naval College. The medium was a railway signalman. Doyle was amazed by some paranormal activity he experienced, but he was no fool, and he considered some other sitters at the séances naive and gullible. Nevertheless, he was intrigued, and he used his deductive skills to investigate the possibility of communion with the dead.

Illustrations

Cover design and chapter illustrations are by Richard C Plaza.
The Skull of Kohada Koheiji – from a print by Katsushika Hokusai c1830.
Three Monks Singing by E H Reed, 19c.

Thanks to Sem Donkers for Dutch translation

The Sherlock Holmes & Young Winston series of
novels and a growing collection of traditional novellas and
short stories are available in paperback and on Kindle –
visit kaleidoscopeproductions.co.uk for details.

The Sherlock Holmes and Young Winston Trilogy

* The Deadwood Stage
* The Jubilee Plot
* The Giant Moles

A review by The Baker Street Society

'There are few if any better pastiche writers at work at the present time....and if you are thinking of writing one yourself, then use these three books as a template, you would not go wrong. Thrills, quite, quite wonderful dialogue between the main characters, well, to be honest between all the characters. There are a few trilogies around, there are a few series around but Mike Hogan's Holmes, Watson and young Winston stand head and shoulders above the rest. Five-star entertainment.'

ABOUT THE AUTHOR

Mike is British and currently lives in Asia. He writes
novels, plays and screenplays. He is an avid Holmesian and
a Monty Python and Frasier fan. His obsessions are
Shakespeare, Ancient Rome and the Royal Navy. Among
his favourite modern writers are Patrick O'Brian, Mary
Beard, Robert Harris, Stephen Ambrose, Rick Atkinson,
Gore Vidal and Tom Wolfe.